DEATH ON TREMONT ROW

A HIGGINS & HAWKE MYSTERY
BOOK FIVE

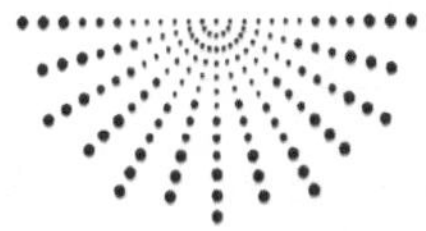

LEE STRAUSS

Death by Dancing

© 2021 Lee Strauss

Cover by Jordan Strauss

Cover Illustration by Tasia Strauss

Library and Archives Canada Cataloguing in Publication

Title: Death on Tremont Row / Lee Strauss.

Names: Strauss, Lee (Novelist), author.

Description: Series statement: A Higgins & Hawke mystery ; book five |

"A 1930s cozy murder mystery."

Identifiers: Canadiana (print) 20230561632 | Canadiana (ebook) 20230561640 | ISBN 9781774093856 (hardcover) | ISBN 9781774093863 (softcover) | ISBN 9781774093832 (IngramSpark softcover) | ISBN 9781774093849 (EPUB) | ISBN 9781774093870 (Kindle) | ISBN: 978-1-77409-475-4 (bookvault) | ISBN: 978-1-77409-476-1 (d2d)

Subjects: LCGFT: Detective and mystery fiction. | LCGFT: Historical fiction. | LCGFT: Novels.

Classification: LCC PS8637.T739 D48 2023 | DDC C813/.6—dc23

NOTE FROM THE AUTHOR

It is true that by the time this book was set in 1932, the area once known as Tremont Row had been changed to the name of Scollay Square, and the road itself to Tremont Street.

Tremont Row has more of a ring to it in my opinion, and I believe that locals at that time would still refer to the area in the way they were accustomed, so I took license to do the same and called this book *Death on Tremont Row*.

THE HIGGINS & HAWKE MYSTERIES

IN ORDER

Death at the Tavern
Death on the Tower
Death on Hanover
Death by Dancing
Death on Tremont Row
Death at King's Chapel

Boston's chief medical examiner, Dr. Haley Higgins, was often accused of working too much. She had a suitable apartment overlooking Grove Street, a nice upper-middle-class neighborhood, which she shared with her friend journalist Samantha Hawke, Sam's young daughter, and a three-legged cat. Mrs. Berrymaple, the widowed neighbor, practically lived there too, hired by Samantha to babysit and by Haley to cook. And though Haley found comfort there, she greatly enjoyed her work at the hospital morgue. Maybe even more so, as it was predictably quiet and she could lose herself for hours studying the latest in forensic medicine. The thirties looked to be a promising decade for scientific advancement.

However, Haley understood that balance in life was beneficial, so she was on her way to see the play *Whispers of Deceit* at the Shubert Theater on Tremont Street.

First, she was picking up her close friend Ginger Reed, who had flown into the Boston Airport from London, England.

Reaching the row of brownstones on Beacon Hill, Haley parked her 1929 DeSoto along the northern edge of the Common. The vehicle, with its flat roof, glossy curved lines, round, bug-eyed headlights, and white-rimmed spoked tires, looked handsome next to the greenery of the vast park.

The brownstone in question had been Ginger's childhood home. Ginger had gone by Georgia Hartigan then and Lady Gold after her first marriage. A lady of fashion and sophisticated flair, Ginger was indeed gold to Haley's silver. Or, more accurately, Haley's bronze. Haley had little interest in fashion or sophistication, but their differences hadn't kept them from forging a strong and long-lasting friendship.

Heading to the front door, Haley paused to pat at her long faux bob, though she wondered why she bothered with anything other than tying her hair back, especially in this heat. Even though it was only May, the city of Boston was experiencing an unusual spike in temperatures, with the mercury hitting the nineties. Her curls were a constant menace, always coming loose, needing repeated pinning. At least tonight, along with her blue satin evening gown—the new styles were more form-fitting than in the twenties, with longer hemlines, and in Haley's opinion, more suitable for her tall figure—and low-heeled leather shoes with the fancy front ties, she felt reasonably put together.

After a breath, she knocked on the door. It was opened by a maid who looked a bit frazzled. Haley thought anyone who spent more than two minutes with Louisa Hartigan, Ginger's much younger half sister, tended to share the look.

"Dr. Higgins, for Mrs. Reed," Haley announced.

"Do come in, Dr. Higgins," the maid said.

Haley followed the maid to the living room, grand-looking with dark wood paneling on one wall, bright wallpaper on the others, tall ceilings, and plenty of electric lights. It had been many years since Haley had been to this residence, and much of the decor had changed, presumably at Sally Hartigan's hand. Ginger's stepmother was an energetic force of nature, and with Louisa, the apple hadn't fallen far from the tree.

"Haley!"

Haley stood as Ginger entered the room, looking almost otherworldly. Glamour and sophistication came easily to some women, and Ginger reigned supreme among them. Her gown fell in sleek waves over a slender hourglass form; her shoulder-length red hair, which always drew the eyes, was pinned expertly on a perfectly shaped head (as a pathologist, Haley noticed cranial structure). Long diamond earrings (and Haley was certain the diamonds were real) hung from deli-cate lobes. Haley would've shrunk into the shadows if she had suffered from a lack of self-esteem. But Ginger had a way of sharing the spotlight with those beside her, and her smile quickly pushed away such thoughts.

"Haley!" Ginger took Haley's arm. "You look fabulous."

"It's you that looks fabulous," Haley said as she embraced her friend.

"We will agree that together, we are fabulous," Ginger said. "Oh, Haley, it's been such a long time."

"Four years since my last stay in London."

"I did mean to come back to Boston before now, but leaving the family for so long is difficult. I'm just happy that Louisa is finally going through with an engagement."

Louisa Hartigan had broken many hearts. Samantha often reported on society events, and Haley was kept up on the latest trail of suitors over toast and coffee at breakfast times.

"This gentleman must have something special," Haley said.

"Mr. Harold Forrester, a successful businessman, made his fortune in railroads and other ventures. Louisa must be truly in love, as she's a real bear now, preparing for her wedding, which is going to take place at Tremont Temple Baptist Church. Sally isn't any better." Ginger lowered her voice. "What a splendid opportunity to go out tonight. Sally and Louisa have kept me busy these last two days since I arrived. Coming so quickly by aeroplane has made me more fatigued than I remember being after a longer journey by ship. That time shift is much harder to adjust to this way."

"I'm just glad you're in town and I'm happy to accommodate your schedule," Haley said. "Are you ready?"

Ginger held out her embroidered clutch purse. "As I'll ever be."

They hadn't quite reached the door when a female voice cried, "Ginger!" Rapid footsteps followed down the stairs. "Ginger, what are you doing? There's still so much to do!" Belatedly, Louisa's eyes registered Haley's presence. "Do I know you?"

Haley smiled widely, the only way she could as God himself had given her a wide jaw. She reached out her hand. "Haley Higgins. I was your father's nurse in his last days. We met again when you and your mother visited London. I was a student at the medical school, taking advantage of Ginger's hospitality."

"Oh yes," Louisa said slowly. "I remember now." Her eyes darted from Haley to Ginger, then narrowed accusingly on Ginger. "Are you leaving me?"

"Just for a couple of hours, love," Ginger said. "It's opening night for *Whispers of Deceit*, and Haley was able to secure tickets."

"They sold out very quickly," Haley added.

Louisa's eyes were piercing at that moment, like a wild goose, and someone who didn't know Ginger like Haley would worry that Louisa could coerce her to stay behind. As it was, she gave it a shot.

"I've seen it," Louisa said, raising her chin. "A preview matinee for dignitaries. It's not all it's cracked up to be. I wouldn't waste your time. The villain—"

Ginger raised a palm. "Don't tell us." She gave Louisa a quick hug before nudging Haley toward the door. "I'll be back before you know it."

As the crow flew, the Shubert Theatre was almost directly south of the brownstone on Beacon Street, just south of the Common. But by motorcar, Haley had to drive around the park and through it on Charles Street to reach the south end of Tremont Street. It was a pleasant drive through the greenery of the parks, the Common to the left and the public gardens with their large pond, a sanctuary for many birds, to the right.

"I can't believe you've been in Boston for three days already," Haley said with a side glance at her passenger, "and this is the first time I've seen you."

Ginger pouted prettily. "Please don't be cross. Louisa's wedding planning has been all-consuming. You've seen her. She inhales all the oxygen from the room, and everyone else is walking around like one of those Haitian zombies in *The Magic Island*." She cocked her head in Haley's direction. "Have you read it?"

Haley shook her head. "No, but I've heard a play, based on the book, opened, or is opening, in New York."

Turning the subject back to Louisa, Ginger continued, "I'm just grateful I'm old and married and don't qualify for the job of bridesmaid."

Haley commiserated, feeling sympathy for the girls who'd agreed to the roles. "Poor dears."

Ginger placed a gloved hand on Haley's arm. "We have so much to catch up on. I am thankful for your letters, but they are not the same as a tête-à-tête. Perhaps we can go somewhere for drinks after the show."

Haley chuckled. "If by drinks you mean coffee or tea, then yes. Don't forget you're now in the land of prohibition."

"Oh bother," Ginger said with a flick of her hand. "What a nuisance."

"I do have a little something stashed away at my apartment, though," Haley said. "We can go there."

"That would be lovely. I'd like to see where you live."

"You can meet Samantha."

"The intrepid lady reporter," Ginger said cheerily. "I can't wait."

HALEY HAD BEEN to the Shubert Theatre before. In fact, she'd been to every theater in Boston at least once, and usually on the arm of Dr. Gerald Mitchell. They'd had a comfortable friendship during the years that his wife had lain in a vegetative state. Gerald remained faithful to his wife while she was alive, but like Haley, he didn't want to attend social events as a single. At least not every time. But once his wife had passed away, he'd expressed a more serious interest in Haley, one Haley found she couldn't reciprocate.

This was why, on seeing him at the Shubert Theatre in the company of another woman, she was confused by her feelings. Her chest tightened along with her jaw. Was she actually experiencing jealousy?

Haley snapped out of her emotional tunnel at Ginger's happy sigh.

"I came here with Daniel once," Ginger said. "When we were courting. It feels like a lifetime ago. So much has happened since."

Haley chuckled. "That's a bit of an understatement. Let's see, you studied at Boston University, married an English lord, moved back to your childhood home in London, volunteered in France during the war, lost your first husband, came back to Boston, went back to London, met and married your second husband, adopted a son and gave birth to a daughter."

"You're no slacker either, love," Ginger said. "Boston's Chief Medical Examiner."

Haley glanced at Gerald and added, "And married to my work."

Ginger followed her gaze. "Do you know that couple?"

"He's a doctor who works at the same hospital as me, but I don't know the woman."

"I don't recognize anyone anymore," Ginger said. "At one time, I could name every socially prominent figure."

Haley had never been amongst the *prominent* crowd, but she did recognize a few faces.

"Is Miss Hawke here?" Ginger asked. "I'm looking forward to meeting her."

Haley craned her neck, searching for a glimpse of her roommate. She didn't find Samantha, but her work colleague Johnny Milwaukee was in attendance. Haley frowned at the sight of his pretty, young date. Though Samantha tried to hide it, Haley sensed her fondness for Mr. Milwaukee was more than just friendliness. Clearly, since the man was on a date with someone other than Samantha, he had different feelings.

"I don't see her," Haley said. "She's probably backstage. I know she hoped to get an interview from Bertram Calderwood before the show."

Ginger pointed at the brochure highlighting all the actors and actresses featured in the performance. "I've never heard of him," Ginger said. "Is he well-known in America?"

"A rising star," Haley said. "At least from what Samantha has to say about him. He's making a name for himself in the talkies. He's doing double duty as a director. Ambitious fellow."

"Veronica St. James I have heard of," Ginger said. "Hollywood silent films are readily available in England. The new talkies are all the rage, but I've not seen them all. What about these other actors and this young actress?"

Haley examined the brochure. Bertram Calderwood

and Veronica St. James played a married couple, Adrian and Evelyn Trafford; Miss Flora Priestley played Clare Wilson, and Mr. Brian House was also part of the cast.

"I haven't heard of any of the others," Haley said. "But I assume they must all be talented to have gotten these roles." She found she was very much looking forward to a relaxing evening getting lost in the play and being proven right.

CHAPTER TWO

Samantha Hawke was used to pushing herself to her limits. She was a single mother to seven-year-old daughter Talia and worked full-time at *The Boston Daily Record*. It could be grueling work, with extended hours—on her feet chasing down stories— but she preferred that to warming a hard chair all day as she had done as the receptionist. Few women worked in her field, and they all had to work harder than the men to justify their existence on the beat. She'd been in the pit at the *Daily* for long enough now to have obtained an alliance of sorts, if not one that had been given begrudgingly.

"Mommy, can you read to me before you go?" Talia shared her mother's looks with honey-blond hair and blue eyes but had the distinction of a missing front tooth.

"Oh, honey, I have to work tonight. Mrs. Berrymaple will read to you."

"She always reads to me," Talia said with a whine. "I want *you* to read to me."

Samantha put a hand on her hip. "I don't appreciate your tone, young lady. Besides, I know perfectly well that you can read to yourself. Now off to bed."

Talia narrowed her eyes, pushed out her bottom lip, and stomped away. Samantha's heart pinched. She wanted to run after her daughter, kiss her head, snuggle into the bed with her, and *read*, but life wasn't fair or kind. Instead, she yelled out, "I won't be late."

Mrs. Berrymaple, the punctual sort, arrived at the agreed-upon time. Although a grandmotherly type, she hadn't had the good fortune of having her own grandchildren. As a childless widow, she was alone in Boston, so her inclusion in Samantha and Haley's affairs benefited them all.

"Don't you worry, Mrs. Rosenbaum," Mrs. Berrymaple said, using Samantha's married name. "She'll be fine. I've got a tin of shortbread to cheer her up."

Samantha offered a smile but didn't know how she felt. She could now afford simple luxuries, like paying a babysitter who brought cookies, while many suffered real hardships. "The show ends at nine," she said. "I'll be home shortly afterward."

Samantha had gotten the gig to cover the opening night of *Whispers of Deceit* at the Shubert Theatre. She'd jumped at the chance when Archie August, her editor, offered it. She'd never been to that theater, or any theater, more than once or twice. Such things had once been beyond her means financially, and it appeared that being frugal had been ingrained. The paper was covering the cost of her ticket for this, so it was silly not to do the job. None of the guys wanted the story. They put it in the same category as the fluff pieces Samantha was required to write for the women's section. Maybe they were right. Her readers would love to hear about the handsome Bertram Calderwood. Samantha would be lying if the idea of interviewing the famous actor didn't give her a small thrill.

"Tell Talia we'll do something together tomorrow," Samantha said, stuffing the guilt she felt down with the rest she carried. She turned to the mirror by the door. Her hair had grown quite long over the past year, now touching her shoulders. She'd swooped the front sections up, used large rollers to get the desired full curl, and pinned her style with several bobby pins. She used a sugar-and-water solution to aid in the setting, which would be sure to hold it in place for the rest of the evening.

Since she was there as a reporter, she hadn't donned an evening gown, as she might've had she been on a date, but that suited her fine. Instead, she wore a two-piece suit, the short jacket resting on the hips while the hem of her split-seam pencil skirt landed mid-calf. Twisting to view the back of her legs, she checked that the seams of her stockings were straight. On her feet, she wore comfortable T-strap shoes, remnants from the previous decade, but still, thankfully, considered stylish.

"Good night, Mrs. Berrymaple," Samantha said before leaving. Louder, she called out, "Good night, Talia. Be good!"

The cabbie drove east along Cambridge, circling south through Scollay until the road turned into Tremont. There was a snag in the traffic, and Samantha's stomach clenched with nerves. She couldn't be late!

Leaning toward the front seat, she spoke to the back of the cabbie's head. "What's the hold up, mister?"

The cabbie adjusted his flat cap. "Looks like an overturned cart, ma'am. You ask me, it's time to get horses off the road. This is the twentieth century, not the Middle Ages." He laid on the horn and shouted out of the window. "C'mon! We ain't got all day!"

Samantha caught the look in the cabbie's eye in the rearview mirror. He didn't look all that broken up to her. The meter was running!

"I'd get there faster if I walked," she said.

"Hold on," the cabbie said. "Looks like the mess is clearing up."

Samantha craned her head, squinting to bring the snarl in the distance into focus. "Traffic's not even moving." They were at a standstill at Temple Place. She really would get to the Shubert Theatre faster if she walked. Pulling bills out of her purse, she handed them to the cabbie. "Take this. I'm getting out here. Keep the change." She could afford to be generous. It was the paper's dime.

Before the cabbie could protest further, Samantha was on the busy sidewalk, hurrying through the crowds, one hand on her hat and the other holding on to the straps of her purse and camera bag. She expertly sidestepped slow movers, even in her heels.

She was breathing heavily when she finally reached the theater. The limestone facade was flush with the neighboring buildings, with ornate round-top windows and inlaid Romanesque columns. Taking a moment to catch her breath, she used a clean handkerchief to pat her brow, then discreetly reapplied her Max Factor brand lipstick in poppy-red.

Smoothing out her skirt, Samantha stepped through the doors, her shoulders back, feigning confidence. She was at the Shubert Theatre! On assignment! Taking in the elaborate decor of the foyer—plush reds and golds—she felt her lips tug into a smile, the only one of the day.

Gripping her press pass, she showed it to the attendant. "*The Boston Daily Record* has purchased my ticket," she said. "I've got permission to go backstage to interview the actors."

The attendant studied an opened notebook on his podium, ran a white-gloved finger down the page, and stopped partway. "Yes, Miss Hawke, I see your name here. Go down that hallway and through the door at the end. It'll take you backstage."

Samantha thanked him and followed his direction, feeling a certain skip in her step and growing excitement in her belly. This was a fun assignment, and best of all, she was getting paid to talk to Bertram Calderwood!

A porter handed her a program for the play, and she took a moment to thumb through it. Along with a full-page advertisement for Lucky Strike cigarettes celebrating their new "toasting" advancements, the program gave a detailed accounting of the play and its three acts, descriptions of all the actors and actresses, and, most helpfully, a diagram of the theater itself.

She turned the handle of an unmarked door to the left of the hallway, but to her surprise, she found herself looking at the back of the auditorium, which hummed with theater-goers finding their seats. The beauty of the stage and seating area took her aback. Like the lobby, it was a splash of extravagant reds, oranges, and golds, as if it had been poured out of heaven during a celestial autumn season. The curtain was a deep red, vertical waves of plush velvet, and the ceiling was sculpted like overlapping shells, gilded in colorful triangular patterns. Beams were painted gold and adorned with white globe bulbs reflecting in a sea of shiny surfaces. Box seating was reserved for the city's elite, with overhead views from the balcony.

Samantha realized that she had taken a wrong turn

and returned to the hallway in search of the correct door that led backstage. When she arrived, a man stood near the entrance and stared at her suspiciously.

"And you are?" he asked.

"I'm Samantha Hawke with *The Boston Daily Record*."

The man's stern expression softened. "I'm Rees Johnson, janitor, and Mr. Kibble's right-hand man."

"Mr. Kibble?"

"The stage manager. This close to opening? You'll see him rushing about like a lunatic."

"I'm looking for Mr. Calderwood and Miss St. James."

Mr. Johnson pointed to the dressing rooms on the other side of the stage.

Samantha thanked the janitor and crossed the area, dodging crew members dressed in black. She found a door with a big star and a sign underneath saying "Bertram Calderwood." She lifted a fist to knock on the door but paused when she heard shouting from the other side.

"You're all wet, Bertie! A no-good shyster," a woman's voice said sharply.

"Ah, don't be dingy, Ronnie. Y'know you're the only filly for me."

"That ain't what Flora's saying."

"Look, don't let her get to you. We got a show in a few minutes. Now hit me with a honey cooler, dollface."

"You'll not feel these lips on yours, Bertie!"

"Ha! You have to kiss me in the show."

"Oooo, you make my blood boil!"

Samantha stepped away from the door just in time to avoid getting hit with it. The lady who stormed through didn't even give her a second look. Hanging on to the belt of her scarlet dressing gown, she stormed to another door with Veronica St. James written on a large black star. She stepped into the dressing room, and she paused for a fraction to cast a seething look at a fellow actress who lurked in the corridor—Samantha recognized the brunette from her image in the brochure as Miss Flora Priestley—before closing the door with a slam.

Miss Priestley made a face before disappearing behind a rack of costumes.

A lovers' spat doesn't bode well for a successful opening night.

A moment later, a young woman bustled out of Veronica St. James's dressing room, looking timid and browbeaten. She caught Samantha's eye briefly before averting her gaze, then hurried away.

"And you thought the play would be the most entertaining thing you saw tonight!"

Samantha turned to the warm male voice. The man leaned against a table, blowing smoke from a half-burned cigarette. He stubbed it out in one of several ashtrays situated around the room. He was dressed casually in cream-colored, pleated and cuffed dress pants, a white shirt with a red tie, and a navy-blue blazer. "You must be the dame from the paper."

"I am," Samantha said, swallowing back the disrespect she felt at being called a dame. "Samantha Hawke."

The man's eyebrows jumped. "You're Sam Hawke?"

Samantha's lips tugged up in amusement. She often got this response from men when they discovered she wasn't a man. "I'm guessing you've read my byline."

"Pretty feisty lady. Going after rum runners like that."

"All part of the job," Samantha said.

"I'd like to shake your hand, all the same. Name's Jethro Maines. I play Greyson Hartley in the play."

Samantha stretched out her arm and shook the man's hand. "Not every story is life and death, Mr. Maines. I'm here to interview Mr. Calderwood and Miss St. James. I hope to do so before the show."

Mr. Maines snorted. "Everyone always wants to talk to them. There's more than those two in this production, ya know. The rest of us aren't small potatoes."

"I'd be happy to interview you when I'm done," Samantha said, hoping to console the actor. She wasn't there to stroke egos but to get the story and do a review. The only person she needed to impress was Mr. August.

Pointing his lit cigarette, Mr. Maines said, "I'd give Miss St. James a few minutes, but Calderwood will be more than happy to give you his time." His eyes scanned Samantha in a way that put her hackles up. "He's fond of tomatoes." He laughed and then clarified. "Good-looking women."

"Thank you, Mr. Maines," Samantha said stiffly. "I know what a 'tomato' is." She hadn't been born yesterday. "By the way, who was that girl leaving Miss St. James's dressing room?"

"That poor thing is Lara Smith, Miss St. James's dresser. Must be like dressing a mountain lion."

Samantha turned back to the lead actor's dressing room door and knocked. Her heart skipped a beat when he called her inside.

Mr. Maines wasn't wrong. Bertram Calderwood's eyes did light up when he saw her.

"If it ain't my lucky day. Come on in, pretty lady, and have a seat."

CHAPTER THREE

Samantha accepted Mr. Calderwood's invitation and took the empty chair in the dressing room. The walls had been papered some time in the past, with the corners near the ceiling beginning to lift. Lit by the row of lights over a makeup desk, the room smelled of strong cologne, greasepaint, and cigarette smoke.

Mr. Calderwood was dressed in an ensemble of comfortable pants and sweater-vest, which Samantha presumed was for his role as Adrian Trafford, the charming if disinterested host of an ill-fated dinner party. Leaning casually against his dressing table, he eyed the pencil and notebook Samantha held. "Don't tell me you're the newshawk?"

"Yes, I'm the newspaper reporter, Samantha Hawke."

A curious smile crossed the attractive man's face. "What will they think of next?"

Hopefully, equality, Samantha thought, though even she, a modern woman, couldn't imagine that happening anytime soon. "I want to say I'm a big fan, Mr. Calderwood. I've seen all your films."

"Thank you." Bertram Calderwood picked up his cigarette case. "Smoke?"

"No, thank you. I'll just ask my questions if you don't mind. I don't want to take up your valuable time."

Mr. Calderwood struck a match and lit his cigarette. "Ask away, Miss News Hawk."

Samantha glanced at her notes. She'd made a list of questions: Did you always want to be an actor? Do you prefer the west coast or the east coast? Why theater after a string of movies?

Samantha suddenly felt that they seemed too well suited for the fluff piece she'd been accused of covering. What she wanted was a real story.

"Have you worked with Veronica St. James before?"

Mr. Calderwood laughed. "You heard that childish outburst? Ronnie is a pill."

"I understand you play a married couple in *Whispers of Deceit.*"

"Aptly, they are unhappy. I'm a good actor, but it would be hard to pretend to be in love with that wench."

Samantha forced her expression to remain still, holding in her shock at his harsh words. She swallowed, then said, "Miss St. James has had a long, illustrious career." Far longer than Mr. Calderwood's. Which made her older than her costar, naturally.

Mr. Calderwood shrugged. "Nothing lasts forever."

"I admit to being surprised that, as the director, you agreed to perform in this play together with her. The bad blood is fairly obvious."

"To you, Miss Hawke, because you're an astute journalist and clearly a student of human character. Regular folk want to believe that Bertram and Veronica are a happy couple in real life."

"The magazines do give that impression," Samantha said. "Someone must be feeding them that line."

"You can thank our agent for that."

Samantha checked her notes. "Mr. Sylvester Hardin? The two of you have the same agent?"

"We do. Hardin thought a pretend romance would lift my star and keep hers high in the sky. And he was right, at least when it came to my star. It rose, but poor Ronnie, hers is sinking like a ship's anchor."

Samantha also noted that the actor didn't insist that anything he said that could be construed as negative publicity be "off the record."

"Again, it begs the question of why you have her as your leading lady," she asked. "Surely, the director has some say?"

Mr. Calderwood sniffed. "Not as much as the producer. Old Mrs. Meadows, our Wizard of Oz, pulls strings behind a screen."

"A lady producer?" Samantha heard the same surprise in her voice as other people expressed when shocked by her role as a woman in journalism.

"She's got the big pockets." Mr. Calderwood shrugged. "Desperate times and all that."

Samantha sensed a theme. This production was on a budget.

A short knock was followed by the entrance of an older gentleman with soft, curved shoulders. "So sorry, sir, forgive my tardiness. The missus is unwell, and I had to run to the market for sleeping powder."

"It's fine, Birnberg."

The man was so focused on his employer that he hadn't registered Samantha's presence right away. "Oh, sorry, miss. Mr. Calderwood, should I come back?"

"Ten minutes."

The man backed out, and Samantha shot Mr. Calderwood a questioning look.

"He's my dresser. It's more of a charity case. I need someone to look after my costumes, but it's easier for me to dress myself."

"I see." After a pause, Samantha decided to hit one of the questions on her fluff list, after all. "How long do you plan on staying in Boston?" she asked.

"Until the play has completed its run." Mr. Calderwood snuffed out his cigarette, creating a substantial plume of smoke. "I'm keen to go back to LA. Not a fan of this heat and humidity, Miss Hawke." He raised a brow. "But since I'm here, I wouldn't mind a tour around your city. Are you game?"

Samantha blinked. Was the rich and famous Bertram Calderwood asking her out?

"Very kind of you to ask," she said, rising to her feet. "I feel it's best to keep things between us as professional as possible. I need to interview Miss St. James now."

Mr. Calderwood flicked his wrist to check his watch. "I fear you're out of time. The callboy's going to be knocking on doors soon, and we actors have to finish getting ready." He smiled his practiced smile. "You'll want to find your seat before the house lights are turned off."

SAMANTHA TOOK Mr. Calderwood's words to heart and hurried back to the theater in search of her seat. Rechecking the note she'd gotten from Mr. August and comparing it to the floor plan in the theater program, she found she'd been allocated a place at the back of the room. With a sigh, she headed back, remembering that she was lucky to be there at all. Thankfully there was a second door to the theater, closer to the stage, that she hadn't spotted before.

She entered through it and was halfway up the aisle when she heard Haley's voice calling "Samantha!"

She waved at Haley, and then her gaze settled on the glamorous lady beside her. Haley hadn't been joking when she described her English friend. The gorgeous red tone of Ginger Gold's hair was certainly eye-catching, and her sophisticated aura radiated outward, hitting Samantha, and creating a wave of low self-esteem. Even though she no longer lived in the tenements, Samantha was still uneducated and uncultured.

Still, Haley was her friend, and any friend of Haley's was Samantha's friend too. Steadying herself with a breath, she smiled and soldiered on, continuing down the aisle until she reached them.

"Haley, hi." Samantha held out her hand. "And this must be Mrs. Reed."

"Please call me Ginger," the lady said with a soft English accent.

"If you'll call me Samantha."

"I've heard so much about you," Ginger continued. "I feel as if we are friends already."

Samantha shot Haley a questioning glance.

"Ginger and I correspond regularly by mail," Haley explained. "Of course I had to tell her about you and Talia."

"Yeah," Samantha said. "I've heard a little about you too, Ginger. I understand you're quite the gumshoe."

Ginger laughed. "Forgive me. I've been away from Boston for some time, and the regional accent is frightfully relaxed. And yes, it's true. I work as a private investigator in London. Haley tells me you're making your mark as an investigative journalist in this city. Bravo."

"Well, I'm here on assignment, so I'm not always investigating."

"Did you meet Bertram Calderwood?" Haley asked, with a twinkle in her eye. "Was he everything you'd hoped he'd be?"

"Not so much hoped, but what I might've expected. I'll tell you about it later, but the show will start soon, and I need to find my seat."

"Join us for *refreshments* afterwards," Ginger said. "Haley's treat at her apartment."

Samantha nodded. She lived there, so she'd be there.

She hadn't gone ten steps when she stopped short at the sound of another familiar voice, this one distinctly male. "You're gonna love this, doll."

Johnny Milwaukee! She pivoted with the toe of her shoe on the carpet, her tongue ready to give him a good lashing about how this was *her* story and he shouldn't try to snatch it from underneath her. But instead, the words caught in her throat when she realized Johnny hadn't been talking to her. He was there, at the Shubert Theatre, with *a date*.

The female twittered, "I promise not to fall in love with Bertram Calderwood, Johnny. At least not tonight, he-he."

Samantha huffed and kept walking, thankful that the lights had dimmed enough that Johnny hadn't caught her staring. What did she care if he was there with a date? Of course he was. If not classically hand-some, Johnny had charm in spades and a string of gals a mile long willing to pant after him. And she wasn't one of those shameless gals. Besides, with Talia and her job, she didn't have time for men, and quite honestly, most weren't interested in an instant family.

It should be easy to shake the dust off her feet when it came to Johnny, but now that Samantha knew his secret, she saw past his devil-may-care, cavalier ways. Finding her seat at the back of the room, Samantha slumped into it. She *was* in Johnny's lineup of gals; in fact, she was standing at the very front of the line.

Utterly in love.

CHAPTER FOUR

The red velvet curtain lifted, and a hush fell across the room. The stage was set to represent a rustic cabin with woodsy furniture, an oval, rope area rug, and a stone fireplace that Haley presumed was made of wood. As Bertram Calderwood entered from stage right, a flutter of whispers from his ardent fans ran through the audience. He faced the dark theater and projected his voice. "Evelyn, darling! Where's the cribbage board? We did pack it, didn't we? Darling? You know how everyone loves a good game of cards."

On cue, Veronica St. James entered, this time from stage left. Again, whispering rippled through the crowd, but it wasn't nearly as vigorous as what had greeted Bertram Calderwood's entrance. "Adrian? What do you mean, did *we* pack it? *You* were meant to pack it. This gathering was your idea. It's your duty to entertain your guests."

"Yes, of course, dear."

The play continued with the rest of the cast joining in, all under the guise of visiting the Traffords at their cottage in the woods for the weekend.

Haley found it challenging to follow the plot of the play. The act preceding the intermission produced such a rapid series of lies and half-truths that by the time the curtain came down, she was certain she was not the only one confused.

Turning to Ginger, she asked, "Do you know what's going on?"

"It's like that game with the pebble under one cup," Ginger answered. "The cups are moving so rapidly that I've lost sight of the pebble."

Haley smiled at the analogy. "There's still the second half of the play. Hopefully, it'll make more sense by the time it ends."

"Shall we get a beverage in the meantime?" Ginger asked. "I'm rather thirsty."

"Good idea."

Haley looked for Samantha while she and Ginger stood in line but didn't see her anywhere. She had probably gone backstage in hopes of another interview.

"Haley!"

Haley turned to the sound of Gerald's voice. Beside him was the woman he'd been sitting with. She was older than Haley and closer to Gerald's age, in her mid-fifties.

"Hello, Gerald," Haley said. "It's good to see you." Haley found that she spoke the words with sincerity.

"Likewise." He turned to his companion. "This is Mrs. Anne Cooper." Mrs. Cooper, presumably a widow, was a natural beauty with perfect bone structure, salt and pepper-colored hair, and notable crows feet around attractive eyes.

"Pleased to meet you," Haley said. Turning to Ginger, she added, "This is my good friend, Mrs. Reed, visiting from London."

As pleasantries ensued, Haley couldn't help taking glimpses of Mrs. Cooper, feeling slightly off balance after seeing Gerald with her. *How long has this friendship been going on?* she thought. *They seem rather well acquainted.* A sharp pang rushed through Haley. Perhaps Gerald hadn't been entirely exclusive when they were stepping out. And why should he have been when she kept blowing hot and cold?

Clearly, Anne Cooper is a better fit for him, she thought, reassuring herself. After all, Gerald made a better friend than a romantic partner, and it was good to have that firmly established.

"Haley?"

Haley responded to Ginger's light touch. "Oh, pardon me, my mind was elsewhere."

Ginger continued to rescue her. "Mrs. Cooper was

just saying that her nephew is one of the actors in the play."

"Is that so?" Haley said. "Which one?"

"Brian House," Mrs. Cooper answered, her eyes sparkling with pride. "He's a vaudeville star, you know. This is another feather in his cap."

"His performance so far has been impressive," Haley offered politely.

The intermission ended, and everyone proceeded to head back to their seats.

"So that was Dr. Mitchell," Ginger said as they settled back in for the next act.

"Yes," Haley said. She'd written extensively to Ginger about her arrangement with Gerald and how things had changed once his wife had died.

"I thought the two of you would . . . you know, when Mrs. Mitchell passed away."

"I thought so too," Haley admitted. "Until it happened. Then it felt strangely forced."

"You seemed taken aback to see him here with Mrs. Cooper."

"Ginger, you're nothing if not astute."

Ginger shrugged a slim shoulder. "It's been mentioned once or twice. Now spill."

"He's free to see whomever he wants; I was just surprised. Not that he'd met Mrs. Cooper, but I sense he's been seeing her for some time."

"Yes, if I recall from the timeline you noted in your

letters, there could be an overlap of time when he was seeing you both."

Haley huffed. "That's what sticks in my craw. Anyway, no matter. We're done, so he can do what he wants."

"And so can you."

The lights dimmed, and everyone grew quiet. Haley let out a slow breath as the curtain rose. She was finished with Gerald. She would move on.

WHILE EVERYONE else headed toward the foyer during the intermission, Samantha, like a fish swimming against the tide, made her way to the stage. After what felt like a hundred mutterings of "Excuse me, pardon me," she broke out of the crowd. With a glance over her shoulder, Samantha pushed through the door that led backstage.

"Excuse me, this isn't a public area."

Samantha turned to the man, who watched her with a scowl.

"You're the stage manager, Mr. Kibble, right? I'm Samantha Hawke from *The Boston Daily Record*. I've been given a pass to interview the cast."

"Dang press," Mr. Kibble said through a puff of cigarette smoke.

"Yes, well, I hope you don't mind, but I'd like to try to sneak in another quick interview, if possible." She flashed a smile, batted her mascara-heavy eyes, and pushed a strand of blond hair behind her ear.

The scowl softened. "Not Miss St. James. She needs to keep her head for the second half of the show. Ya know, showtime ain't a great time to be botherin' the talent. I'd wait until after if I were you."

Just then, Flora Priestley walked by, a glass of water in her hand. Samantha, ignoring Mr. Kibble's admonition, scrambled after her. "Miss Priestley. I'm with *The Boston Daily Record*. Would you like to say anything to your fans?"

Miss Priestley froze, wide-eyed. "Would I! Oh, my goodness, a real newspaper reporter wants to speak to me? Yes!" She glanced around, her smile faltering slightly. "I don't have my own dressing room. Yet. But there's a quiet spot over there."

Samantha followed Miss Priestley to a corner where props were lined up against a wall, then, with pencil poised over her notepad, asked, "I understand you had to compete with many other actresses for the role of Clare Wilson." Samantha didn't know about the process but expected an answer either confirming or correcting.

"Well, not so m—" Miss Priestley stared ahead, her countenance changing into what Samantha would call her acting face. "Actually, yes. Many others. It was such an honor to win the role."

The lie was obvious—rising to the top of a large pile of actresses clamoring for the role was more newsworthy than beating out a few wishful thinkers—but Samantha scribbled Miss Priestley's desired answer in her notes. It wasn't like the piece on the play was meant to be a serious recording of facts. Its role was to entertain.

"Is it true that you were born and raised in Boston?" This much Samantha had learned in her cursory research.

"Yes," Miss Priestley said with her plastic smile, "but I've worked very hard on my accent to sound Midwestern. You couldn't tell, could you?"

Having been born and raised in Boston herself, Samantha could hear a hint of the Boston accent a mile away but shook her head politely.

"So, what's it like working with professionals like Mr. Calderwood and Miss St. James?"

"Mr. Calderwood is the bee's knees. I'd love to star in a talkie with him someday. Any actress would."

"And Miss St. James?"

Miss Priestley's smile fell. She made a show of looking at her watch. "Oh, look at the time! I really have to visit the ladies before the curtain call." Her phony smile returned. "It was marvelous speaking with you, Miss . . ."

"Miss Hawke," Samantha offered.

"Miss Hawke." Miss Priestley wiggled her fingers. "Enjoy the rest of the show!"

Samantha felt a surge of frustration. She'd hoped to have her interviews completed before the show's end so she could leave immediately for home. With only two interviews, she'd have to return backstage and corner Miss St. James. She and Mr. Calderwood were the winning ticket to get readers to buy the paper, and Mr. August would be disappointed if she didn't get something from the difficult actress.

Samantha had to watch the whole play to report on it properly. It was a convoluted affair so far. She probably wouldn't give it high marks if she were a critic. But maybe the ending would change her mind.

She'd just turned toward the exit when Brian House, the actor who played Miss Priestley's love interest, blustered into the backstage area, slamming the door behind him. "Dumb broad!"

Mr. House stuttered to a stop when he spotted Samantha, his handsome face holding on to his frown. He glowered when his eyes rested on the pencil and notebook in Samantha's hand. "You'd better not print that or I'll sue for defamation."

Samantha held out a palm. "I'm not looking for scandal, Mr. House, but if you provide one for free, well, it's a free press."

Mr. House huffed and disappeared behind stage gadgets.

"Don't mind him," Roy Kibble said with a coy grin. "Brian House is too big for his britches—mad at the world that he's not more famous than Calderwood."

He stubbed out a cigarette at the sound of the callboy's voice, "Five minutes to curtain! Second act begin-ners, five minutes!"

It was Samantha's signal to find her seat.

"You love her, don't you? Admit it!"

Adrian Trafford lets his fists fall from his hips. "And what if I do? I'm doomed to unhappiness, tied as I am to you?"

"You're unhappy?" Eleanor Trafford marches around the kitchen, her hands gripping her hair. "I'm the one being made a fool of!"

"Keep your voice down," Adrian says tersely. "We have guests."

Eleanor looks at her hands with wild eyes and laughs, low and throaty. "Is one of them warming up her bed for you?"

"Eleanor!"

"See here." Eleanor reaches for the carving knife drying in the dish rack. She holds it out to her husband. "If you're so unhappy, why not end it now?"

"Don't be absurd," he retorts. "You're acting like a lunatic."

"You're not the only one who's unhappy, Adrian." She turns the knife on herself, placing the tip on her abdomen.

Adrian stares back with contempt. "You're too vain and conceited to actually knock yourself off."

"You don't think I'll do it?"

With a shake of his head, Adrian says, "No."

"Well, watch this."

Eleanor falls onto the table, the knife pushing in to the hilt.

"Eleanor!" Adrian runs to her side, catching her as she collapses; a blood-red splotch blooms across her white blouse.

THE LIGHTS DIMMED as the crowd gasped. The curtain fell. In the darkness, a loud, hoarse outcry resounded.

CHAPTER FIVE

$\mathcal{H}$aley jumped to her feet and turned to Ginger. "I don't think that was part of the play."

Scooting past the other patrons, Haley and Ginger expressed their pardons, ignoring the slighted glares and looks of disbelief.

"Such cheek," one lady said. "Leaving at the most exciting part of the play."

"Haley!"

Haley turned to the sound of Samantha's voice. "I saw you get up."

The three women rushed in front of the stage, the muffled sounds of crying and words of distress reaching them from the other side of the curtain.

"Sam, how do you get backstage?" Haley asked.

"This way." Haley and Ginger followed Samantha through the door to the backstage area. A frazzled-looking man with hair falling across his forehead put a palm out when he spotted them. "No one's allowed back here!"

Haley stepped to the fore. "I'm Dr. Higgins. Is someone in need of medical attention?"

The man eyed Haley in the way she had grown to expect—not with appreciation of feminine beauty, which Haley never aspired to, but with suspicion that a woman should have such important credentials.

His brow arched. "You're a doctor?"

"I am."

"Very well, you might as well see this. Got ourselves a real problem." He stared back at Samantha. "But not you. No hacks."

"Whatever happened here, Mr.—"

"Kibble. I'm the stage manager." He pushed the wayward hair off his face. "Oh dear. This is all just so terrible."

"Mr. Kibble," Haley said calmly, "whatever happened here will reach the press. If you want fair and truthful coverage, I vouch for Miss Hawke." Besides, Samantha had a camera, which Haley intended to put to use.

"Very well." Mr. Kibble stared at Ginger, and this time his eyes registered appreciation. "And who's this dame?"

"This is my colleague, Mrs. Reed, a first-rate investigator. Now, Mr. Kibble," Haley said with authority. "Please lead me to the patient."

Mr. Kibble muttered something about what the world was coming to as he guided the three ladies to the stage. "'Fraid it's not a patient, Doc, but a victim."

Haley shared a quick look with her companions. It was quite clear that Veronica St. James was no longer among the living. "Have the police been called?" Haley asked.

"Just finished doing so when you entered the back," Mr. Kibble replied.

"We don't have much time," Samantha said to Haley under her breath. She patted her camera bag. "Should I?"

Haley nodded. "Please."

Bertram Calderwood raised two hands when he saw them. "Hey, what's this?"

"I let them in," Mr. Kibble said. "The tall one's a doctor."

Mr. Calderwood's shoulders slumped in resignation. Haley felt the man wasn't used to being in situations where he wasn't in control.

Flora Priestley sat in one of the prop living-area chairs and sniffled into a handkerchief. Jethro Maines leaned back against the same chair, arms folded. Brian House straddled one of the wooden ladder-back kitchen chairs.

Veronica St. James lay on the floor beside the long edge of the table, the handle of a kitchen knife standing erect from her abdomen. The actress's hair was mussed and her skin a gray-white. Her eyes were round and open, the shock of her death still apparent in her unseeing gaze.

"I recommend that nothing be touched or moved before the police arrive," Haley said. "Quite clearly, the play will need to be stopped. Mr. Kibble, I'm afraid you have the unenviable job of informing the attendees that the night has ended abruptly."

"There will be a riot," Mr. Kibble said. "Mrs. Meadows will be furious."

Haley raised a dark brow. "Mrs. Meadows?"

"The producer," Mr. Kibble explained. His face darkened with an unpleasant afterthought. "I suppose they'll want their money back. This is a disaster."

Samantha, who was busy preparing her camera, caught Haley's eye. Haley gave a slight nod in acknowledgement. The manager seemed more upset at the thought of losing money than about having a dead actress on his stage.

Jethro Maines pointed at Samantha. "Should she be taking pictures? I mean, isn't that the police's job?"

Haley answered for both of them. "We work in tandem with the police. I wish I had my doctor's bag," she muttered as she knelt on the ground by the body. From her peripheral vision, she could see Ginger slowly moving about the stage, no doubt taking in every little detail.

From the angle of the knife entry, Haley noted it would've entered through the anterior of the heart.

"I thought they used prop knives," Samantha said as

she prepared her camera. "The kind where the blade slides into the handle."

"Me too." Haley studied the weapon around the hilt. "It looks like it might've been jimmied. I'll have a closer look at the lab."

Haley got to her feet. Seeing Ginger waiting behind her, Haley asked, "Did you notice anything strange or unusual?"

"Not on the face of things," Ginger said. "But I thought you'd like to know that the police have arrived."

Haley looked beyond her friend, expecting to see Detective Cluney's familiar, heavyset form, but she was surprised to see a face and stature she didn't recognize. Unlike Detective Cluney, this man was tall—a head and shoulders above every other man in the room—slender and had a pleasant look. He wore a light overcoat and a fedora, dented on the front left, and Haley wondered if the man had a habit of bumping his head on low and sloping ceilings. A step behind him was Constable Thomas Bell, who usually accompanied Detective Cluney.

"I understand we have a body on the premises," the man said confidently. "I'm Detective Nolan Brock."

Haley stepped forward and extended her hand. "I'm Dr. Higgins, the city of Boston's chief medical examiner. You must be new."

"Indeed, from Delaware."

"Where's Detective Cluney?" Haley asked with sincere curiosity.

"He went on vacation with the family."

"Oh?" Haley had known Detective Emmet Cluney for a year and never heard him speak of taking a vacation. It was long overdue. Still, others on Boston's force could've covered for him. Why Detective Brock was standing before her and not one of them was a question she'd have to save for when Detective Cluney returned.

"I've heard all about the lady medical examiner," Detective Brock said. "It's a pleasure to meet you finally. Kinda like meeting a mythical fairy."

"Pardon me?' Haley said, unsure if she should be offended or not.

"You know, a creature one hears about but never sees. You don't know if it's real or not."

"I'm very real, I can assure you, Detective, as is this body at our feet."

"Ah yes, the situation at hand." Detective Brock tugged on his trousers and squatted.

Haley glanced at Samantha and Ginger, who both stared at the new detective, the first with school-girl admiration, as the detective, Haley would have to admit, was attractive, and the latter with bemusement.

CHAPTER SIX

Haley watched as Ginger approached the detective with her gorgeous smile. "Detective Brock, I'm Mrs. Reed, a good friend of Dr. Higgins. I'm here as her guest, but I'd like to excuse myself if it's all right with you. You see, my family is waiting. Dr. Higgins can instruct you how to reach me if you need me."

In Haley's experience, Detective Brock behaved like most men did in the company of the delightful Ginger. His jaw slackened as he first processed her charm and beauty and then, after considering the fact she was married and out of reach, mentally stepped away.

However, Detective Brock quickly overcame his initial primal instincts and proceeded professionally. "I'm certain that will be fine, Mrs. Reed. Are you visiting from England?"

"Yes," Ginger said, "though I lived in Boston for

some years as a girl." To Haley, she said, "I believe you're about to have a long night. Do ring me tomorrow when you have a chance." She then said goodbye to Samantha before gliding off the stage, with everyone watching as she went.

"I admire your ability to be friends with her," Samantha said. "I think I'd shrink a little from intimidation and the constant feeling of falling short."

Haley smiled. "I did feel that way at first, but Ginger is hard not to love. And she has a lot of substance, far more to credit her than simply her outward beauty."

Everyone's attention returned to the corpse of Veronica St. James.

Of no one in particular, Detective Brock asked, "You're telling me the actress offed herself onstage in front of hundreds of onlookers?"

Bertram Calderwood answered, "Committing suicide was part of the play. It's just like her to make a spectacle and to actually kill herself. She'll certainly be the talk of the town now."

The detective approached the actor. "You don't seem particularly broken up."

"How would you know how I feel?" Mr. Calderwood said defensively. "We're not all going to show our emotions like Miss Priestley."

Miss Priestley glared at Mr. Calderwood, then made a show of blowing in a very unladylike manner into her handkerchief.

"Everyone is to remain for questioning," the detective said. Then to Haley, "I'm assuming you can declare the cause of death?"

"Obviously, she was stabbed, blade running upward in a sharp angle under her ribs. But the cause of her death was cardiac arrest due to a penetrating cardiac injury. The I can confirm once the autopsy has been completed."

"When it suits you, you may arrange for the body to be removed," Detective Brock said, "then you and your journalist friend are free to go."

"Thank you, Detective," Haley said.

Samantha spoke to Haley out of the side of her mouth. "Johnny's trying to weasel his way back here. Constable Bell is refusing him entry."

"Mr. Milwaukee's not happy about that, I suspect," Haley said.

"I'll stay as long as I can get away with it. I can't pass up this opportunity for a scoop. Thank goodness for Mrs. Berrymaple, who is always so willing to watch Talia."

"We'll both get booted out soon enough," Haley said.

As the police continued their investigation and securing of physical evidence, Haley returned to the stage and found Mr. Calderwood standing in the back.

"What's happening now?" Haley asked him.

"Interviews in Kibble's office. Kibble is in with the detective now. The rest of us are just supposed to wait around for our turn."

"I see," Haley said, hoping to sound sympathetic. "Such a shame, all of this. And I was so enjoying the show."

Bertram Calderwood cast her a glance of indifference.

Haley appealed to the man's vanity. "Your performance, in particular, was captivating. You're a real talent."

Mr. Calderwood smiled back crookedly. "Kind of you to say so."

"In my profession, I deal with people suffering loss all the time," Haley said. "Grief looks differently on everyone. If I were to go by the reports in the rags, I'd be led to believe that you and Miss St. James were very close. You've done several plays and films together."

The actor harrumphed. "A contract bound us, nothing more. Ronnie is, um, *was* a complicated woman. Not the easiest to work with. Not that I wanted her to die," he added quickly.

"It's rumored that the two of you were more than just collaborators on film and the stage," Haley said.

"Once upon a time, I thought we had a chance at romance, but the first time we went out in public, she nattered on and on about some guy named Dean."

"Dean?"

"Yeah, some guy she used to date. She kept comparing him to me—how I was more of a gentleman than Dean. I was a better dresser than Dean, smarter, more talented, blah, blah. A guy loves to be praised, don't get me wrong, but by the end of the night, I wanted to bop this Dean guy in the nose."

"What happened to Dean?" Haley asked.

Mr. Calderwood shrugged. "I heard he kicked the bucket. I guess she really wanted to join him."

"You believe this to be suicide?"

Bertram Calderwood gave her a surprised look. "What else could it be?"

"Murder, Mr. Calderwood."

Mr. Calderwood laughed. "I saw her stab herself with my own eyes. Hundreds of people did. Including you."

"It's my understanding that you can't actually harm yourself with a prop knife."

"Ronnie must've swapped it out. I wonder how long she'd been planning this?"

Before Haley could respond, the door to Mr. Kibble's office opened, and a frazzled-looking stage manager walked out. "Next."

"I'll go," Mr. Calderwood said, shooting a look to the stage where the others must've been waiting. "Best to get this over with so I can return to my hotel. I wonder if Sly's been notified."

"Who's Sly?" Haley asked.

"Sly Hardin, our agent. Um, my agent."

As Mr. Calderwood disappeared into the office, Haley headed to the stage to find the other actors. The new detective had assumed that she'd left with the body and probably wouldn't take it kindly when he found out she'd remained behind to mingle with the suspects, but she'd deal with him later.

SAMANTHA LET herself into the apartment. She and Haley had decided it would be best for her to go home, develop her film, and start writing up the story. Haley would continue the investigation. After checking on Talia, who was sound asleep, and releasing the kind-hearted Mrs. Berrymaple to return to her apartment next door, Samantha picked up the kitchen telephone and asked the operator to connect her to Archie August's home telephone. Her editor didn't mind being interrupted at home if one of his "men" had a good story to report.

"What?" came Mr. August's dry, gruff voice.

"Mr. August, it's me, Samantha."

"I hope there's fire or blood, Miss Hawke."

"Blood, sir. A death at the Shubert Theatre."

"The play you're covering?"

"Yes. The lead, Veronica St. James, is dead. It appears she committed suicide in front of hundreds of patrons."

The editor whistled loudly, forcing Samantha to pull the receiver from her ear as she winced.

"Did you get photographs?" he barked.

"I did, sir." Samantha had agreed with Haley that she'd be permitted to take photographs at the crime scene as long as Haley viewed them first. It was a given that nothing graphic would be published.

"Get them developed and write up the story. I'll head to the paper now. Gotta get this in the morning's edition!"

Samantha's heart raced, and the palms of her hands tingled. She had a scoop, but she had to be quick about things. She hurried to the bathroom, where a red lamp had been installed so the room could be used as a darkroom in moments like this. She ran the film through the developer and fixer solutions before washing it thoroughly, then hung it up to dry, pinning it to a line across the bathtub. With the photographs processing, she started on the story. She had an extra typewriter at home, which she carefully and quietly removed from the bedroom she shared with Talia and positioned on the kitchen table.

Veronica St. James, 38, a silent film and stage actress, is dead.

In a climactic scene, life followed fiction. Not to spoil the plot, but St. James's character comes to an untimely end. However, it wasn't a case of acting in last night's show.

Boston's chief medical examiner, Dr. Haley Higgins, happened to be attending the performance and was one of the first on the scene.

The question remains: was it a dramatic suicide or a sinister murder?

Samantha worked her lips. She needed to be careful not to write anything that could be construed as interference by the police. Or by Haley.

Her tag might smell of sensationalism, but Samantha reasoned that it would be the question on everyone's mind, at least eventually. She submitted a photograph she had taken while the play was in progress from the position granted to her at the front of the stage. A good one of Veronica St. James not long before her death. Haley would have no issue with that, and hopefully, Mr. August would be appeased.

Samantha continued writing: *More on this story to come as it unfolds.*

HALEY HAD to step around a man leaning on a broom. "Pardon me," she said. "I'm Dr. Higgins."

"I know who you are," the man said. He had a soft voice and the kind of nondescript appearance of a person easily overlooked. "I've heard you introduce yourself a few times already."

"Are you the custodian for the theater?" Haley asked with piqued interest. Janitors were often the quiet sort who knew more about the people they worked for than those very people would be comfortable knowing.

"Rees Johnson at your service, ma'am. I'm also the janitor at Tremont Temple Baptist Church."

The same church Louisa Hartigan was soon to be married in, Haley thought, noting the coincidence. She was thankful for that information, for as much as she wanted to question the janitor, she wanted to speak to the actors and get to them before the new detective would think to stop her.

"Nice to make your acquaintance," she said.

"Likewise, ma'am."

Haley found Flora Priestley, Brian House, and Jethro Maines sitting morosely on set pieces on the stage, as far apart as possible. Mr. House was the closest to Haley, so she headed for him first. The actor was average in height and looks, with nothing striking about him to turn the head, the kind that often got the part of the friend.

"Mr. House, we haven't officially met—"

"You're the lady doctor."

"Yes, pathologist, actually. I had the pleasure of meeting your aunt this evening."

Mr. House glanced up. "Auntie Anne was here? Don't tell me she came with that old man."

Haley couldn't help but blink back her astonishment. Gerald wasn't *that* old; he was only in his mid fifties. Maybe his gray hair made him look ancient to this upstart in his thirties. And Mrs. Cooper wasn't a young chick either.

"She was in the company of a gentleman," Haley said. "A friend of mine."

Mr. House gave her a condescending nod. "Well, they got more than they bargained for, didn't they? Such bushwa. Now we're all out of a job." He chortled derisively. "No one is safe from the soup line."

"It's a tragedy, for sure," Haley said. "Did you know Miss St. James very well? Aside from time spent rehearsing this performance."

"If I did, why should I tell you?"

"I'm just making conversation, Mr. House." Haley leaned casually against the back of a couch. "An event like this must be hard on the nerves, even for an experienced actor like yourself."

"Yes, well, I spent years as a vaudevillian actor—as a kid, my family was a group of travelling troubadours— and then, when I finally broke into film, talkies started, and somehow, I once again ended up at the bottom of the pile. This was supposed to be a step up for me. She promised."

"She?" Haley motioned with her chin toward the spot where the body had been found. "Do you mean Miss St. James?"

Brian House flapped an arm. "Yes. She was the boss lady around here—Mrs. Meadows's pet. And the dumb broad owed me a favor. She promised me the lead. Gave it to Calderwood instead. Next time, she said. Always next time. Now, *Doctor*, I'm waiting to be interrogated by the police. I don't appreciate being questioned by you as well."

"My apologies," Haley said rather insincerely. "Please give your aunt my regards."

Haley intended to speak with Miss Priestley next but was interrupted by the presence of Detective

Brock, who, for some reason, decided not to send his constable to call the next actor.

"Dr. Higgins?" he said with a barely suppressed scowl. "What are you doing here?"

"Just offering a bit of comfort," Haley said.

Behind her, Brian House scoffed.

"All the same," Detective Brock said, "this is a police investigation. I will call on the morgue in due time."

This public dismissal was a little embarrassing, but Haley took it in stride. "Of course, Detective." With her shoulders back, she turned to leave, giving Constable Bell a little nod. He, at least, had the decency to look contrite. Detective Cluney would never have treated Haley this way.

CHAPTER SEVEN

*H*aley sipped her morning coffee as she read the newspaper. Above the fold was Samantha's byline. "Oh," Haley said after reading it.

"It's the question," Samantha said, looking a little eager. "Too much?"

"Well, it's true," Haley said. "It's either suicide or murder. Miss St. James either purposefully rigged the knife to go out with dramatic horror, or someone else did it for her." She checked her watch. "I need to get to the morgue and start the postmortem."

"I need to face the pit," Samantha said, referring to the room at the paper she worked in with the other reporters, who happened to all be male. "The guys hate it when I scoop a story." She chuckled. "Hard cheese."

Haley lifted her cup in salute. "That's the spirit."

"Talia!" Samantha called as she smoothed down her slender-fit floral-print skirt, which had a mid-calf hem and was belted at the waist. The matching blouse had short, flouncy sleeves, a bow centered on her collar. She looked both feminine and professional with her black patent leather heels and a felt side-up-brim hat. "Sweetheart, are you ready to go?"

THE MORGUE in the basement of the Massachusetts General Hospital was a short drive north from Haley's Grove Street apartment, though, with the increase in morning traffic, it often took less time to walk. Since the weather was pleasant, Haley left her '29 DeSoto parked at the curb and cut across Cambridge. By the time she headed into the hospital basement, she felt invigorated by the sunshine and fresh air.

She was greeted by her younger assistant, who'd apparently just arrived. He was hanging up his coat and hat when she walked in.

"Hello, Dr. Higgins," he said, running his hand over his oiled hair and then drying his hand on a white handkerchief.

"Hello, Dr. Martin," Haley returned. "I'd like to get started on the body that came in last night."

"I'll pull it out of the cold cupboard and get it ready."

Haley settled into her office, reviewing the paperwork that accompanied the body. She glanced through the wall of glass windows that looked out onto the operating area. Painted a bright white, the morgue had a clean, open feel, and with the advent of electric lighting, the staff no longer had to count on the small, high-set windows and dangerous oil or gas lamps.

Once Dr. Martin had the body on the white porcelain surgical table, Haley went to the wash station to wash her hands and don a white apron.

"I can't believe I missed last night's performance," Dr. Martin said. "We had tickets and everything, but Mitzie came down with something and was too ill to go."

"It was a spectacle." Haley waved a hand. "What happened to the knife?"

"It's right here." Dr. Martin held out a tray with a bloodied knife lying on it. "The woman had the gall to do such a thing," he said. "It's not easy to go through with stabbing yourself."

"She fell onto the table," Haley said. "I'm not convinced the knife wasn't jimmied." Retrieving a magnifying glass from a drawer, she had a closer look. "The latch that was meant to give has been disengaged. There are tiny scratch marks, probably created by the small tool used to do it."

"Detective Cluney will want to see that," Dr. Martin said.

"Ah, here's more news for you, Dr. Martin. Apparently, Detective Cluney is on vacation."

Dr. Martin raised a brow. "Vacation?"

"That's what I said. A Detective Nolan Brock is on this case."

"And why don't you like him?"

"I didn't say I didn't like him."

"Not with words."

"Good Lord. Don't tell me you can read my mind now," Haley huffed. "Please pass the scalpel."

THE AUTOPSY CONFIRMED that Veronica St. James had died as a result of a laceration to the right ventricle. She would've gone into shock before dying moments later. Alcohol had been found in her blood—liquid courage to help her go through with suicide? Or just a matter of course for someone who was fond of drinking?

"I'll let you stitch her up," Haley said. She washed her hands but still wore the bloodied apron when Detective Brock's entrance followed a brief knock on the door. Haley blinked back her surprise. Not that the police never came to the morgue for information, they did, but she hadn't counted on a visit so soon. Haley was also disgruntled by the flash of vanity she felt, looking quite unbecoming, she was sure, in front of this handsome man who grinned at her like he knew he had the upper hand.

"Dr. Higgins," he said, removing his banged-up fedora. "I've caught you off guard."

"Not at all," Haley said stiffly. She removed her soiled apron and tossed it into the laundry basket. She smoothed her skirt but refused to tend to the loose curls around her face. "It's a shame you didn't drop in earlier. You could've watched the show."

The detective's brown eyes darted to Mr. Martin, who was earnestly stitching up the Y incision. "Seems I've caught the last act."

Haley stepped into his line of vision. Though Mr. Martin had covered the body with a sheet, there was a chance the detective might see more than Haley would like, and she wanted to protect Miss St. James's dignity, even in death.

"Is there something I can help you with?" Haley heard the terseness in her voice. She'd felt slighted the night before as if she and the detective weren't on the same team. She folded her arms and raised her chin.

Detective Brock took a step closer. "I feel like we got off on the wrong foot yesterday. You know, first-day-on-the-job blunders."

"Why would you say that?" Haley asked, relaxing her arms. "You were merely doing your job."

"As were you." Detective Brock rocked on the heels of his leather loafers. "Even after the body was removed, apparently. Cluney told me what a big asset you are to the department and that I'd be wise to keep you on my side."

"Detective Cluney said that?" Haley said. The burly man wasn't known to offer up compliments. "Wait, I thought he was on vacation?"

Detective Brock reached for the back of his neck.

"Um, well, not exactly a vacation. He's here in the hospital."

Haley felt a surge of concern. "Is he all right?"

"Appendicitis. He's kinda embarrassed by it."

"Appendicitis is painful and certainly nothing to be embarrassed about."

"He's a proud man," Detective Brock said. "Thinks it makes him look weak." Chuckling, he added, "A guy would feel that when flat on his back like that and at the mercy of the nurses."

Haley folded her arms again. "You seem very well acquainted with Detective Cluney."

"Here's where I confess. He's married to my mother's cousin. So, we're kind of related. Through marriage."

Haley raised a brow. "Is that why you got this case?"

"I was already hired—on the force in Boston for a month now. I suppose it's just chance we didn't meet before, or probably because I wasn't yet working homicide. Anyway, like it or not, I'm my uncle's replacement. For this case, anyway."

Haley started for her office, and the detective fell into step behind her. "Is there something you'd like to ask me?" she said as she claimed her desk chair.

Without invitation, Detective Brock helped himself to a wooden chair, folding his long legs like a cricket. "There is. Would you go out to dinner with me?"

Haley failed to keep the shock from her face, her jaw growing slack. The man staring back at her had a lot going for him. He was ruggedly handsome, relatively intelligent, presumably single, and taller than her, which was a nice change.

She gathered her wits about her. "No, thank you. Anything else?"

Detective Brock leaned back, blinking in surprise. Clearly, he wasn't used to getting turned down by the gentler sex.

"May I ask why?"

"I like to keep my professional life separate from my work life. You are firmly assigned to the latter."

"I see. Very well, I'll move on to my next question. Is there anything of note to report from the autopsy of Veronica St. James?"

"Nothing I hadn't expected to find," Haley said. "Heart damage. However, you should take a look at the knife." She retrieved the tray and presented it to the detective. "It hasn't been cleaned yet, but you can see it's been sabotaged."

Detective Brock held the tray close to his face and squinted. "Yes, I see the widget has been jimmied." He settled his dark eyes on Haley. "Is this something Miss St. James could've done herself?"

"I suppose," Haley said. "In your experience, Detective, have you ever had a case where someone successfully stabbed themselves to death?"

The man shook his head. "It's rare. The natural response is to stop at the point of pain, resulting in an injury, certainly, but not full penetration bringing on death."

"She did fall onto the table," Haley conceded, "but even so, her reflex would be to twist away unless she was under some hallucinatory influence. I'll have to wait for the laboratory results to find out if Miss St. James had drugs or alcohol in her system."

Detective Brock spun his crooked fedora on his long index finger. "See, that's why I came to see you, other than to apologize, of course. My gut says murder."

"Based on your interviews with the cast?" Haley asked.

"None of them was completely honest with me," the detective said. "I've got an inkling for such things like truth-telling. So, I have to ask myself, why?"

"Do any of them have motive?"

The detective smiled as he got to his feet. "That's what I intend to find out."

"What did the props master have to say?" Haley asked. "Mr. Kibble, wasn't it?"

"Yes, also acting stage manager. The fellow was flustered, to say the least. Too much on his plate, I reckon, though he wouldn't admit to it. Said the prop knife functioned properly when he put it in the kitchen drawer on the set." With a quick bow of his head, he returned his dented hat to it. "It's been a pleasure, Dr. Higgins."

As abruptly as he had entered, the detective left.

Haley didn't have long to muse about the man as the telephone rang. Since Dr. Martin was busy returning Miss St. James's corpse to the refrigerated cabinets, Haley answered and was pleased to hear Ginger's voice on the other end.

"I'm dying to know what happened," she said without preamble. "Care to join me on a trip to Filene's Basement? You can fill me in."

"Filene's Basement? Since you know I don't shop unless it's absolutely necessary, I'm not sure why you're asking".

"A little birdy told me that one of the cashiers there also worked as a dresser for Miss St. James while she was in Boston performing at the Shubert Theatre."

"Ah," Haley said. "You know, I do have a hankering to go shopping after all."

CHAPTER EIGHT

When Samantha arrived at her desk in the pit at *The Boston Daily Record*, housed in a three-story stone building on Water Street, Johnny Milwaukee and the boisterous sports writer Fred Hall were in a heated discussion over politics. Not that that was anything new. Since the crash and subsequent depression, even previously non-political people had strong opinions.

"He's taxing the poor!"

"He has to add taxes to help the poor."

"Mark my words, Hoover is on his last legs."

Samantha blocked it out as she hung her jacket on the coat rack. Her gloves and purse went into her desk drawer, then she made a beeline to the editor's office, passing the picture of President Lincoln on the wall on her way.

Archie August waved a lit cigar toward Samantha

when he saw her. "Hawke, good, come in." He stabbed the paper before him with a stubby index finger, pressing it against the story she'd submitted. His lips pulled up crookedly. "Good work on the suicide or murder angle."

"Thank you, sir."

"Were you dabbling in sensationalism, or is there some merit?"

"I don't believe it's an open-and-closed case, sir, if that's what you mean."

"Your doctor friend said so?"

"She implied it," Samantha said carefully. "I'll call her to see if she'll confirm the case is still open."

"What about that new detective?"

"I can call him too."

"See if you can scratch up a follow-up story."

Samantha bit the inside of her cheek to keep from smiling. Finally, she wasn't automatically tasked with a fluff piece for the women's page. "Yes, sir."

Mr. August waved her off as he blew a plume of scented smoke into the air.

Samantha's time in the editor's office had been noticed, and the roar of the pit momentarily dulled as she came back in. She walked confidently, her eyes averted, knowing what the men saw—a stylish woman determined to succeed. She'd come a long way from the gal who had to adjust the style of her clothes with safety pins and scrape the bottom of her lipstick tube for the last vestiges of color.

Her upward change in circumstances had come at an odd time—when the rest of the city, the country, and the world was facing sharp downward economic changes. She had her late husband Seth and his possibly illegally obtained inheritance to thank for that, but she'd never forget where she came from and what it was like to struggle. Nor was she under the impression that she'd never fall into dire straits again. She remained frugal and empathetic to those who were suffering.

"Hey, doll."

Samantha turned to Johnny's voice, and to her chagrin, her heart skipped a beat. "Hey," she said, keeping her focus on her desk.

Johnny didn't take the hint and sidled up to her, leaning casually on her desk, as he often did, staring down at her with curious eyes. "Nice suicide piece. You must've burned the candle late into the night."

"I was in the right place at the right time."

"I was there too."

"Not on assignment, though." She caught his eye. "Who's the new lady?"

"Ah, you saw that, huh?"

"It wasn't hard with the lights on. If you were trying to hide her, you didn't do a very good job."

"Yeah, well . . ." Johnny pushed off the desk. "Such as it is, I can't hang around to chitchat. Since Franz von Papen became chancellor of Germany, that Hitler fellow has been gaining popularity. I'm sure there's a real story there."

Samantha wrinkled her nose at Johnny's back as he strolled away. She had a *real* story. Especially if the actress had been murdered. Samantha picked up the telephone on her desk, a reward Mr. August had given her after she and Haley had helped the police solve a difficult and dangerous case. To the operator, she said, "Please put me through to Dr. Higgins in the city morgue."

After a few moments, Dr. Martin spoke. "Sorry, Miss Hawke. Dr. Higgins just left to go shopping with Mrs. Reed."

Samantha stared at the telephone receiver. Had she heard the morgue assistant correctly? *Haley shopping?*

After thanking Dr. Martin, Samantha tried the police department. She had better luck reaching Detective Brock.

"Ah, yes," came his response when she identified herself. "The blond lady reporter."

Samantha silently retorted *Just* reporter *would do.* "That's right," she said instead. "You might've seen my byline in this morning's edition of *The Boston Daily Record.*"

"As a matter of fact, I did, *Sam Hawke.* The question is: was it suicide or murder?"

"Well, that is the question, isn't it?" Samantha returned. "And the crux of my call. Have the police or you come to a conclusion? Was Miss St. James murdered or did she take her own life?"

"You know, I'm feeling kind of hungry. Why don't you meet me for a sandwich, and we can discuss it in person."

"I'll buy my own sandwich."

"That was assumed."

"Okay then," Samantha said. "Name the place."

She hung up and gathered her coat. Her gaze caught Johnny, who was watching her from across the room.

"Hot date?" he asked with a smirk.

Samantha wasn't sure how things had got off the rails between them. She was sure they had shared a moment when she was recovering in the hospital after suffering an injury in a previous case. But, after a couple of weeks back in the pit, things cooled. She didn't know if she had subconsciously pushed him away out of guilt or if he was the one who had gotten cold feet. But nothing had ever been talked about, and now they were back to quips and competition over stories.

"Nothing so interesting as that," she said noncommittally. She was glad the detective had picked a sandwich shop a good distance from the paper, as she'd hate for Johnny to stumble upon them accidentally.

THE SANDWICH SHOP wasn't much for charm, filled with rows of tables, each accompanied by four chairs, and the standard row of stools along the counter down one wall, and a row of booths along the other. But what it lacked in charm, it made up for in quality, and the reputation was obvious: nearly every table was taken. She searched the faces, mostly male, focused on their coffees and sandwiches and briefly wondered if Detective Brock had yet to arrive. Then she saw his long arm reach above all the heads and wave at her.

"I ordered you a chopped corned beef sandwich; I hope that's okay," the detective said. "I figured corned beef would be safe, eh? And coffee. We're both on the clock."

Samantha had no preference and appreciated the man's respect for her time. She slid into the booth opposite the detective. "Sure. That's fine with me."

"I sprang for the extra nickel to get it toasted." Detective Brock pushed the cream and sugar toward her, his dark eyes lingering on her face briefly.

Men usually looked at Samantha in one of two ways: appreciation mixed with a bit of lust, or disinterested contempt. The first was for obvious reasons, and the second was because she dared to enter their world as an investigative reporter.

Detective Brock was an exception. His look was of curiosity and intrigue.

"You're good friends with Dr. Higgins," he stated as he added sugar to his coffee. "And Dr. Higgins is good friends with the attractive redhead that was part of your trio, but you and she aren't that well acquainted."

Samantha stared back in shock. "You're very intuitive."

Detective Brock's mouth lifted in a half smile. "It's a job requirement. So, why did you want to meet?"

"I would think that's obvious."

"Still, I'd rather not guess or assume mind-reading abilities."

Samantha sipped her coffee before saying, "As you know, I'm working on the story about Miss St. James's death, and something tells me she didn't off herself."

Detective Brock raised a brow. "Is that so?"

"You're not the only intuitive person in Boston, Detective."

"I suppose not."

Samantha inclined her head. "So?"

"You expect me to spill police business? For your rag?"

The waitress arrived with the corned beef sandwiches, giving Samantha time to think about how to respond. "I suppose there's no point in denying that that's exactly what I want. I'm a working girl with a daughter to support . . ."

Detective Brock looked up over his sandwich.

"I know I'm called 'Miss,' but I'm a widow. Many men don't like a married woman working, even if their husbands are gone. Maybe we can help each other."

"How can you help me, Miss Hawke?"

"Folks talk to me in ways they won't talk to the police. I'm an investigative reporter, so I sometimes come across interesting information before the police do. And I work with a lot of loud-mouthed reporters. I hear things."

Having said her piece, Samantha picked up her sandwich and took a small bite. The flavors of the roasted meat, along with mayonnaise and horseradish on the toasted bread, were satisfying, especially on an empty stomach.

Detective Brock wiped mustard from his lip. "So, a you'll-scratch-my-back-if-I-scratch-yours type of thing."

"Yeah, something like that."

"Whatcha got?"

"Well, I interviewed all the actors before the play, for starters," Samantha said. "Except for Miss St. James."

Detective Brock looked back with interest. "That is something, I reckon. What can you tell me about Miss St. James?"

"She was a fading star, and none of her collaborators seemed to like her. In fact, she and Bertram Calderwood were having a terrible fight when I got backstage. Everyone could hear it."

Having wolfed down his sandwich, the detective used a wooden toothpick to scrape at his teeth. "Is that so? They all swore love and respect for the woman when talking to me."

"If that's the truth, they have a strange way of showing it." Samantha leaned in eagerly. "So, Detective? Was it murder?"

"How long have you known Dr. Higgins?"

Samantha shook her head at the sudden change of subject. "We met a year ago."

"Hit it off right away?"

"No, not really. We ran in different circles, you could say."

"She seems like the type who tends to keep people at arm's length."

"Intuitive again," Samantha said with a nod.

After a sip of coffee, the detective asked, "How'd you break in so fast?"

"Our jobs caused our paths to cross, and we nearly died together on one occasion. Why the interest in Dr. Higgins?"

"I think she's beautiful."

Stunned, Samantha laughed. "I think she's beautiful too." Though Samantha knew Haley didn't share this opinion about herself.

Samantha hummed. Haley would definitely not approve if Samantha meddled in any way. On the other hand, Haley had been unlucky in love. Maybe Detective Brock was just the man to change Haley's fortunes.

"We'll continue 'scratching each other's backs?'" Samantha asked.

"I don't see any harm in it. Catching a killer is the most important thing. I'm not so proud to say I could use help occasionally. I know women like Dr. Higgins don't like to feel pushed or rushed, so let's keep my intention between us for now. Agreed, Miss Hawke?"

"Agreed."

The detective checked his watch. "I need to get back to the precinct." He stared at Samantha's half-eaten sandwich."

"Go ahead," Samantha said. "I don't mind finishing alone."

"Good day, Miss Hawke. Until we meet again."

"Good day, Detective." Samantha watched the man walk away and giggled. Detective Brock, with his abrupt and direct manner, couldn't have been more different from Dr. Gerald Mitchell, Haley's former gentleman friend. And maybe that was why he had half a chance with Haley. Opposites attracted, and Samantha had a good feeling about those two. Call it intuition.

Wondering what to do next, Samantha found herself thinking about the mysterious producer, Mrs. Sophia Meadows. It aggravated her that she hadn't asked Detective Brock about her when she'd had the chance. She wouldn't let that stop her, though. Referring to a telephone book in the nearest phone booth, she found an address in Back Bay, then waved down a taxicab.

THE CABBIE STOPPED at a regal residence on the west side of the Public Garden, which overlooked the

Charles River. Evidently, Mrs. Sophia Meadows, an uncommonly wealthy widow, enjoyed a quality of life not known by many in the city. Samantha took a chance that the lady's curiosity would override the fact that a journalist was calling on her without an appointment. Climbing the white steps to the heavy wooden door, she pressed the doorbell. A maid answered, and Samantha introduced herself.

Left alone in the entryway as the maid inquired, Samantha took in the extravagance of the marble floors, high ceilings, electric chandeliers, and many gold-framed paintings hanging on walls papered in green and white stripes.

The maid returned shortly. "The mistress will see you."

Samantha followed the maid into a parlor that looked to be straight out of a magazine. An ornate fireplace—unlit during this extraordinary heat—with matching wood-trimmed settees and armchairs arranged in a semicircle facing it. The room had wall-to-wall carpeting, something Samantha hadn't ever seen before in her life, and more framed paintings hanging on a wall papered in smoky-blue paisley.

A slip of a woman sat in one of the armchairs and stared at Samantha with a look of intrigue. "A lady reporter?" she said. Her eyes were the deep blue of the river, enveloped by folds of skin and watering slightly. She had bold cheekbones and a full mouth, evidence of former beauty. Her skin was translucent, papery and white like onion skin. Samantha thought Mrs. Meadows might be the oldest living person she'd ever had the privilege of meeting.

They weren't alone. A man with a large briefcase and a serious expression sat at a small table.

"Do sit down, Miss Hawke," Mrs. Meadows said, then instructed her maid to bring tea. She turned her attention to Samantha, who'd taken the second armchair. "Before we start, I wonder if you'd do me a favor."

Samantha blinked back her surprise. "If I can."

"I'm revising my will, and I need a second witness. Would you mind?"

Before Samantha could answer, Mrs. Meadows motioned to her lawyer. "Mr. Fenster, please provide Miss Hawke with a pen."

Samantha only carried a pencil, so she accepted the pen when offered. The lawyer discreetly covered the will's contents with a sheet of paper, only revealing the space where she was to sign. "My legal name is Rosenbaum," she said, glancing at Mrs. Meadows. When the lady shrugged with indifference, Samantha signed.

The lawyer shuffled his papers and stuffed them into his briefcase before leaving.

The tea had arrived, and after Samantha had been served, they both took a moment to take a sip. Then Mrs. Meadows started, "I've lived a very long time and have seen the world change. I never thought I'd see the day where a woman could be more than a mother and wife or a spinster who's either a teacher or a nurse."

"It's a challenge, all the same," Samantha said. "We women aren't welcomed warmly, even now."

"And probably never will be, but we need women like you to blaze a trail. If I'd been born in a more modern time, I would hope I would do something extraordinary. Become a professor or an engineer." Mrs. Meadows blinked slowly. "Or a reporter, like you."

Where her body was weak, her mind was sharp, and Samantha couldn't help but wonder if such an intelligent mind had been wasted because it was housed in a female body.

"I married well," Mrs. Meadows continued. "At least if one were to measure wellness in terms of finance. Mr. Meadows was a difficult man to live with, a keen mind for business, but had not an ounce of empathy. No one shed a tear when he died, not even me. We had been married for twelve years when his heart gave out, and I've been a happy widow ever since, going on fifty years!"

Samantha blinked back surprise at such an overt revelation of the lady's intimate past.

"I've always been fascinated with theatrical arts." Mrs. Meadows smiled, revealing teeth that seemed too long, time having been unkind to her gumline. "Of course, in my day, actresses were considered women of ill repute. Interestingly, *actors* were never given the same salacious reputation. As a lady of means and status, I could only become involved as a patron. And that only since the turn of the century when societal opinion softened, partly thanks to the advent of film."

"I understand you were the producer of *Whispers of Deceit*," Samantha said. "How did that come about?"

Mrs. Meadows paused for such a long time, Samantha thought the elderly lady might've forgotten what they had just been talking about, but then she said, "Miss St. James approached me, God rest her soul. I envied her youth and beauty."

To Mrs. Meadows, Samantha thought, everyone must be young. "So, you liked her then?" At the elderly lady's confused expression, Samantha expounded. "I'm afraid most people I've talked to about her did not."

Mrs. Meadows sipped her tea. "Is that so?" she finally said. "I have to admit, she lived life with flair. I confess I haven't lived with such courage for many years. I'm waiting for the good Lord to take me as he wills."

Samantha noted that the producer didn't actually answer the question. "Did you get to know the other cast members?"

"Oh, I met them all, of course."

"What do you think of them?"

"You're asking me for character references?" Mrs. Meadows sniffed. "They're all charlatans. Actors, by nature, can't be trusted. They *act*. But I suppose that's what I find thrilling. Being a play producer is like being an animal tamer in the circus, except that I use money to get them to do as I wish instead of a whip."

Samantha felt a slight ripple of fear at the elderly lady's confession. Had she paid off one of the actors to do her "will" and kill off her star?

"What will happen to the play now?" Samantha asked. "Will you lose money on it?"

Mrs. Meadows waved a frail hand. "The play will go on, I suspect. I can afford to lose money, but those actors and that agent cannot."

"Are you referring to Sylvester Hardin?" Samantha asked.

"Yes, that lump of lard. If there ever was a gold digger, it's that man. I wouldn't put it past him to kill off a problem client, especially when the sensation would bolster the reputation of a new, younger, pretty one."

Samantha sipped her now tepid tea. Mrs. Meadows's age and social status seemed to give her freedom to speak in such a way that Samantha herself hadn't learned to enjoy.

"Thank you so much for your time, Mrs. Meadows. This visit has been very enlightening."

Mrs. Meadows leaned on her cane. "I hope that when I'm gone, you'll write a sensational piece about me." She smiled as the plethora of wrinkles around her mouth deepened. "Perhaps you should come for another visit in the future, and I can relay the story of my life. It's quite entertaining."

"I would love that," Samantha said with sincerity.

As she exited the producer's building, Samantha pondered everything the lady had revealed and walked to the nearest phone booth. A worn telephone book hung from a wire, and Samantha flipped through the pages until she got to the names starting with *H*. Running her gloved finger down the page, she stopped when she got to Sylvester Hardin. Could that be Sly Hardin, the agent?

She dialed the operator and recited the number. When the operator put the call through, it was answered by a man with the rough voice of someone who had smoked many cigarettes for a long time. "Hardin!"

"Is this Sly Hardin, the agent?"

"The one and only, ma'am."

"I'm Sam Hawke from *The Boston Daily Record* . . ."

"Oy, Sam, you need to smoke a few cigars and deepen your voice. Ya sound like a dame."

"Mr. Hardin, Sam is short for Samantha."

"A lady reporter?" His accent was pure Bostonian as he pronounced reporter as "repotah."

"Yes," Samantha said wearily. "There's more of us around than you think."

"All right, what can I do for you, *Miss* Hawke? No, let me guess. This is about Veronica St. James."

"It is. I was at the play last night and am working on the story for my paper. I'm hoping you'll agree to see me."

"Ya know, normally I wouldn't, but I gotta see you with my own eyes." He laughed. "A lady repotah! I'm here for the next houwa; then I'm out."

He ended the call before Samantha could get his location. She found the address in the telephone book and hoped the agent hadn't recently changed his office's location.

CHAPTER NINE

"**I** can't believe how much Boston has changed since I left," Ginger said. "It's been nine years since I was last here, so I really shouldn't be so surprised."

"What's the biggest change?" Haley asked as she maneuvered her DeSoto into a parking spot near the corner of Washington and Summer, a block off Tremont Street.

"Scollay Square was called Tremont Row back then."

"Many people still refer to it as such," Haley said. "It's hard to change people's habits."

"I'll always think of it as Tremont Row," Ginger said with a nod of understanding. "There are many more buildings now, fewer horses, and unfortunately, more men looking down and out."

"You've described most cities in the modern world."

"I'm happy that Filene's still exists as it always has."

"Though the Basement is more popular now."

Filene's Basement was where the bargains were found, and by the lines going in and out, discounts were more popular than ever.

Haley and Ginger went into Filene's main entrance, considerably less crowded, and found someone who directed them to Lara Smith. She had shadowy circles under her eyes and stood behind the counter with slumped shoulders.

"Miss Smith?" Haley said as they approached. "I'm Dr. Higgins, and this is my friend, Mrs. Reed. I was the physician in the house at the Shubert Theatre last night. I understand you were Miss St. James's dresser?"

"I was," Miss Smith said, her chin lowering defensively.

"I'm sorry for your loss," Ginger offered.

"We weren't close. I work here during the day, but I only get half-time hours. Working nights at the theater helps to keep the lights on. I was only going to be working with Miss St. James until her play ran its course, then another play and another lead actress would come along."

"So, you didn't follow Miss St. James from project to project?"

"I wasn't her personal assistant. If I had been, I wouldn't be working here. Now, unless you wanna buy something, I'm busy."

Flicking through a rack of dresses, Ginger pulled

out a deep blue satin gown with flattering vertical seams and a daring neckline. "This would look fabulous on you, Dr. Higgins. You are coming to the wedding, aren't you?"

"I think I lost the invitation," Haley said, knowing she'd never got one in the first place.

"Oh, you simply must come," Ginger returned. "As my personal guest." She held the item out to Miss Smith. "Before you ring that up, perhaps you wouldn't mind answering a few questions the good doctor has."

Miss Smith's eyes darkened in conflict, and Haley guessed she weighed the risk of losing the sale over cooperating.

"Sure," she said, taking the dress. "What do you want to know?"

"What was Miss St. James like?" Haley asked.

Miss Smith snorted. "I'm afraid I can't use such a word in public."

"You didn't like her, then?"

"She was a miserable cow. No one liked her, but I'm sure you've learned that much already."

"If she was so difficult, why did you work for her?"

"Like I said, it was a job." Lara Smith held up the garment that now sat on the counter. "So, are you buying this or what?"

The next stop for Haley and Ginger was Tremont Temple Baptist Church, a short drive down Washington and north on Tremont Street. The church didn't look like the standard fare with a steeple and grave-yard. It was one of a series of buildings nestled side by side on the street, the former Tremont Theatre with a facade in the Renaissance revival design, with only an arched doorway and a cherry-red awning to draw attention. The huge sanctuary had rows of pews facing an altar under high, ornate ceilings. Balconies with more pews ran along both side walls. A pipe organ took up most of the back wall over the choir.

And because of Louisa's imminent wedding cere-mony, the sanctuary was a hive of activity, with florists attaching decorative ribbons and flower bouquets to the ends of all the pews, installing large flower arrangements behind the altar, and placing an exces-sive number of candles in candelabras in strategic locations.

Louisa and Sally were there. "Ginger!" Louisa said. Her cheeks were flushed red with the exertion of ordering the hired helpers around. "This is a surprise."

"A little late to be of much help," Sally muttered. Her cheeks were drawn, and her eyes had a hint of dark circles. She glanced at Haley and Ginger wearily, and Haley got the impression that when the whole affair was over, Sally would be happy and finally have some peace and quiet with Louisa out of the way for a while.

"We're actually looking for the janitor, Mr. Rees Johnson," Ginger said.

"I think I saw a man with a broom," Sally replied. "Check the foyer."

Haley and Ginger did just that and found the quiet man in the supply closet, which had a cross hanging on the wall along with the brooms. When Haley noticed a black Bible on the shelf, she thought that maybe it wasn't so strange for a man of faith.

His eyes warmed with recognition as they settled on Ginger. "You're the sister of the bride. I thought I recognized you at the Shubert Theatre."

"Yes, the bride is my sister," Ginger acknowledged. "I'm Mrs. Reed. I'm also a good friend of Dr. Higgins, who attended the scene when Miss St. James died."

"A shame," the janitor said.

"Mr. Johnson, did you see anything unusual at the play?" Haley asked.

Mr. Johnson leaned on the handle of the broom. "I'm not sure what you mean, Dr. Higgins."

"Did anyone act strangely?"

His full lips pulled up slightly. "Stranger than usual? Ma'am, actors, in general, are a strange bunch."

"Mr. Johnson, were you and Miss St. James on friendly terms?"

"Oh no. I wasn't worthy of any relationship with her." He lifted his broom. "I'm a *janitor*."

Haley had learned that Veronica St. James could treat people she thought beneath her in a demeaning way. Had the janitor borne the brunt of it? "Mr. Johnson, Miss St. James was murdered." She paused, waiting for his reaction, but he gave her nothing.

Quietly, he said, "I thought she killed herself."

"It was a theory, at the beginning. Do you know of anyone who might've wanted Miss St. James dead?"

"I can't tell you anything I haven't already told the police," Mr. Johnson said. "Mr. Kibble might be more helpful."

"The stage manager?" Ginger asked.

"He's the stage *and* the properties manager. Everyone's cutting corners these days." He shrugged. "He was in charge of the prop knife."

CHAPTER TEN

The office of Sly Hardin, on Tremont Street, was a smaller hole-in-the-wall affair with a door that was easy to miss. In fact, Samantha did walk by the nondescript entrance until it was clear she'd passed the building number in question and had to double back.

The door creaked as it opened to a small lobby littered with discarded newspapers. The door on the right had a handmade sign that read *Hardin Agency*. She knocked and stepped inside after "Enter!" was bellowed from the other side of the door.

In a word, Sly Hardin was *round.* He had a round body and a round bald head, with big round eyes that looked exaggerated with the thick lenses of his round wire-framed spectacles. Samantha had to pinch her lips together to keep from laughing.

"So, you're the lady reporter, huh?" he said, waving

to an empty chair. "Good-lookin' too. Have you considered a career in actin'?" He smirked, managing to hang on to the cigar that flopped in the corner of his mouth. "I'm down an actress now."

Samantha crossed her ankles and poised a pencil above her notepad, determined to stay professional. "Thank you for seeing me, Mr. Hardin. Would you mind telling me how long you've acted as Miss St. James's agent?"

"Since she was a teenager. She was my first client. I made her a film star, ya know. She wasn't quite Clara Bow but had star quality for a while. I want to say the talkies were her downfall, but the truth was she got old. Like we all do. Hollywood wants a fresh young face, ya know."

"Mr. Calderwood is also your client."

Mr. Hardin bobbed his head. "Top of my roster. I'm pinning my retirement on him."

"I understand that he and Miss St. James were contracted to work together."

"Yes. It's what the public seemed to want. Definitely what the studios wanted."

"Did *they* want it?"

Mr. Hardin scoffed as he squished his cigar out on an over-full ashtray. "I wouldn't say that. But business is business."

"You knew Miss St. James well. Did she seem like the kind of person who'd kill herself?"

Frowning, Mr. Hardin shook his head. "I wouldn't

have said so. But, ya know. Ya think you know someone and pfft."

"Is it possible she didn't take her own life?" Samantha asked carefully.

"Whatcha mean? Wait, you think she was murdered?"

"Not only me, Mr. Hardin, but the chief medical examiner as well."

"I'll be danged." Mr. Hardin rubbed his bald head with a beefy palm. "Well, I'll be."

"Can you think of anyone who'd want her dead?"

"Look, Miss Hawke. Miss St. James was a fiery gal, all right, entitled and demanding, and so she could rub people the wrong way, see. It could be anyone, I suppose, but not me. She was my bread and buttah. I wept when I heard she died. Saddest day of my life."

Samantha didn't doubt the man grieved over a loss of income, but he hardly showed signs of regretting that Miss St. James no longer walked this earth.

"What's going to happen to Mr. Calderwood now?"

"Whatcha mean?"

"He's obviously freed from any contractual obligations that he had with Miss St. James," Samantha said. "Does he have something lined up to do without her?"

"Well, he's still got the play."

"The play?"

"Yeah, *Whispers of Deceit* at the Shubert Theatre."

"I assumed the play would close now that they've lost their star actress."

"Oh no." Mr. Hardin pushed up on his round glasses. "My new client, Flora Priestley, is taking the role."

"Flora Priestley?" Samantha couldn't keep the shock from her voice.

"She was Miss St. James's understudy, didn't ya know?"

"It hadn't come up," Samantha said. "I'm sure she must be ecstatic,"

"Oh, she is. I just talked to her on the phone. She's on her way over."

THE ENTRANCE of an exuberant Flora Priestley followed an excited rap on the door. Samantha hardly recognized the actress because her brunette locks had recently been bleached to a very pale blond. She was so focused on her agent that she didn't even notice Samantha sitting there.

"Hello, Mr. Hardin! We're gonna make a great team!"

Mr. Hardin's round eyes grew wider as he nodded in Samantha's direction. "We're not alone, Miss Priestley."

Flora Priestley paled. "Oh, sorry. I didn't see ya there."

"Do you know Miss Hawke?" Mr. Hardin said. "She's with the papers."

"Ya, she was there when, ya know, Veronica . . ."

"This is a serendipitous turn of events for you, isn't it, Miss Priestley?" Samantha said dryly.

"*Serend*—what?"

"With Miss St. James gone, you get her role. How lucky."

"Yeah, well, it's not like I haven't worked hard for it." She folded her arms defensively.

"No one's saying otherwise," Samantha returned. She softened her tone, wanting the actress's cooperation. "I'm covering the story of Veronica St. James's death. I'm hoping you can help."

Miss Priestley casually crossed her legs, taking a moment to examine her manicure. "Sure. Why not?"

"How well did you know Miss St. James?" Samantha asked.

Miss Priestley shrugged. "Not very well. I only met her a few weeks ago when I got the part of Clare Wilson."

"What were your impressions of her?"

"I don't know. What does it matter what I thought of her? It's not my fault she decided to off herself like that. Mighty bold of her, I'd have to say."

"Do you know anyone who might've wanted to harm Miss St. James?"

Miss Priestley stilled. "Are you asking if she had enemies?"

"Did she?"

After a scoff, Miss Priestley said, "A ton, I'm sure. Veronica St. James was full of herself, if you know what

I mean. She was a self-appointed queen bee. Everyone was to be at her beck and call, and if she decided she didn't like someone, she'd cast you out of the hive. We were all on eggshells around her." She paused, then added, "Except Bertram."

"What did Miss St. James think of you?" Samantha asked.

"I don't suppose she thought much," Miss Priestly said, "and I didn't care what she thought. What's this *really* all about, anyway?"

Mr. Hardin laughed. "I was thinkin' the same thing, but I get it now. Ya think me and Miss Priestley were in it together? I get rid of a losin' asset in exchange for a more promisin' one, and Miss Priestley gets her dream?"

Samantha lifted a shoulder. "Murders have been committed for less likely reasons."

"Murder?" Miss Priestley's head spun to her new agent. "What's she talkin' about, Sly?"

Miss Priestley's shock looked sincere to Samantha, but then again, Flora Priestley *was* an actress.

"Seems our Veronica might not have killed herself."

"But I saw her do it." Miss Priestley cast a glance at Samantha. "So did she. So did a lot of people."

"I have it on good authority that the knife had been tampered with," Samantha said.

"Golly gee." Miss Priestly's voice was like air easing out of a balloon. Then, with a look of distress, she turned to Mr. Hardin. "You don't think the rest of us are in danger, do you? Sly?"

"Darlin', you're worryin' too much," Mr. Hardin said. "This is all speculation, I'm sure. Besides, if someone did kill Veronica, it was personal. He's not after you."

"Can't say I'm surprised," Miss Priestley said definitely. "But don't look at me, Miss Hawke. I didn't kill her. If anyone was sick of her and her antics, it was Mr. Kibble. She owed him money."

Samantha raised a brow. "I would imagine that someone of Miss St. James's stature and fame would have plenty of money."

"Yeah, well." Miss Priestley lifted her chin. "She must've spent it."

Mr. Hardin focused his round eyes on Samantha. "Now, Miss Hawke, what will you write about in your paper? I'll have you know I've got good lawyers, so you be careful not to slander me or my client."

"My story is about Veronica St. James," Samantha said, standing. "Thank you again for your time. I'll let myself out, as I'm sure the two of you have a lot to talk about."

As Samantha strolled down Tremont Street, she wondered if the ambitious Miss Priestley would do anything for a role, even murder. Samantha waved down a taxi and instructed the driver to take her home. She was eager to talk to Haley and share notes on the case.

CHAPTER ELEVEN

After Haley and Ginger spoke to Rees Johnson, Ginger said she would stay behind. "I fear I've elicited Sally's wrath by neglecting familial duties today."

"Cheers, then," Haley said.

"See you tomorrow!" Ginger returned cheerily. "I wish I could keep investigating with you, but alas, needs must."

Haley smiled at her friend's British colloquialisms. "I promise to update you next time we get a chance."

Haley slid into the driver's seat of her DeSoto and drove north on Tremont, intending to take a left onto Cambridge and circle back home. It'd been a long day, and Haley daydreamed about whatever scrumptious dinner Mrs. Berrymaple might be assembling.

Fortune had different plans. She'd only just passed King's Chapel Burying Ground when she spotted

Jethro Maines walking furtively along the sidewalk. With a glance over his shoulder, he tugged on the brim of his hat and disappeared into a stairwell.

Haley pulled her car over and parked. There was a common explanation for what she'd just seen. Speakeasies popped up and shut down and popped up again all over the city, like a field of groundhogs; this was probably another one of them.

Hurrying to the stairwell, she made her furtive motions, taking care that no one was watching her, then slipped into the stairwell. When she knocked, a small door in the larger door opened, and a set of mean-looking eyes stared out.

Channeling Ginger's acting skills, Haley smiled and twisted a curl around one finger. "I'm supposed to meet a gentleman here. I'm so silly. I forgot the password."

"You're not with the police?"

"Oh no. I'm all in favor of a little hooch now and again. Please, mister. I'm really thirsty right now."

It seemed that Miss Flora Priestley wasn't the only actress left in town. The man opened the door and let her in. It wasn't the first speakeasy Haley had been to, and this one shared many of the same characteristics with the others. The music, played by skilled Black musicians, was jazzy and loud. Cigarette smoke obscured the vision and burned the eyes, scantily dressed bar girls delivered drinks, and a few carefree folks danced on the floor in front of the stage.

The bouncer kept his steely gaze on her, and Haley

thought it prudent to buy a drink and quickly prove she wasn't there to cause trouble.

With a sidecar in hand, she turned from the bar and headed to a table where Jethro Maines sat alone. She'd spotted him as soon as she'd entered, but he'd been too focused on his drink to notice her. However, when she took a seat across from his, the look of surprise on his face was no act.

"Wh—"

"Hello, Mr. Maines," Haley said with a smile. She raised her glass. "Mind if I join you for a drink."

"How did you—"

"I saw you walk in. Don't worry. I think prohibition agents are starting to give up."

Mr. Maines regained his composure. "I'll play. What are you doing here, Dr. Higgins?"

"Same thing as you, I suspect."

Mr. Maines raised a brow. "Somehow, I doubt that."

"All right. I'm hoping you can talk to me about Veronica St. James."

"Rather morbid, talking about the dead, isn't it? But then again, you must like morbid things, bothering to get into your line of work and all that."

Haley felt called to her profession and saw herself as an advocate for the dead—those who could no longer speak for themselves. It was why she'd risked following Mr. Maines into an illegal establishment.

Instead of defending her choices, she said, "It was a spectacular way to go."

Mr. Maines took a long sip of his drink. "Grisly, that. Can't imagine what possessed her. Rather risky, too, eh? What if she chickened out and in front of all those people."

"Actually, I have reason to believe Miss St. James didn't kill herself."

"Murder?"

"Does the concept surprise you?"

Mr. Maines shrugged. "Miss St. James was somethin' in her day, but she was a withering rose. She didn't like it and, as a result, made everyone she knew suffer. Really, it could be anyone."

"Even you?" Haley prodded.

Mr. Maines laughed. "I've got a delicate stomach. If I were going to off someone, it wouldn't involve blood. Or witnesses."

"I'll keep that in mind."

Mr. Maines' attention was drawn to someone over Haley's shoulder. His eyes lit up like Ginger's husband Basil Reed's when Ginger walked into the room, or as Samantha's did when she thought no one saw her looking at Johnny Milwaukee.

Haley turned, curious to see what young lady had captured Mr. Maines, only to find a gentleman staring back with a look of bewilderment. He caught Haley's eyes for a split-second before pivoting on the toe of one shoe and walking to the bar.

Mr. Maines coughed into his fist.

Haley sipped her drink. She didn't wish to make

Mr. Maines uncomfortable, but she was fairly certain she knew why he'd never shown any interest in her or prettier girls like Samantha. However, if he failed to show a proud woman like Miss St. James the kind of attention she expected and even demanded—well, like the man said, she could've made him suffer.

CHAPTER TWELVE

*H*aley was grateful that she and Samantha were home for the evening. They'd had a pleasant dinner together, stew and biscuits, compliments of Mrs. Berrymaple, and Talia was now tucked into bed.

"Join me in the living room? I'll make tea," Haley said. It was too late for coffee, but after all the time she'd spent in England, she'd learned to appreciate a good cup of tea.

"Yes," Samantha said enthusiastically. "I've got a lot to tell you, and I want to hear about your day, too."

The living room of Haley's Grove Street apartment felt rich and cozy. Decorated in deep burgundy and dark woods, the room was accented with houseplants, including a miniature palm. Tall windows of the corner apartment added natural light during the day, and in the evening, since electricity hadn't been added to this room, it was brightened by candles or oil lamps. In the winter, the fireplace added warmth.

"You go first," Samantha said.

"Detective Brock came to the morgue first thing this morning," Haley said.

"Is that so?" Samantha's eyes widened in surprise, a reaction Haley found perplexing. It wasn't unusual for members of the police force to visit her. Though it *was* unusual to be asked out by one, at least so soon after meeting. Haley decided to keep that part of her retelling to herself.

"His gut feeling is that Miss St. James was murdered, which, as you know, my evidence supports."

"I saw Detective Brock today as well," Samantha said. "We conferred over lunch."

"Lunch?" Haley felt herself scowl. Detective Nolan Brock hadn't taken long to move on from her refusal. And why shouldn't he after she so quickly and decisively turned him down? Haley only wished he hadn't moved on to Samantha specifically, though she really didn't have a right to dictate who Samantha should or shouldn't see."

"Haley? Are you all right?"

Haley snapped back to attention at the sound of Samantha's voice. "Yeah, sure. Was your lunch date productive?"

"It wasn't a date," Samantha said. "He left before I did, and I paid the twenty-three cents for my sandwich. It was just a way to kill two birds with one stone."

Haley didn't know why that admission made her feel better. She had nothing to do with the detective's dating or eating schedule. "What did he say?" she asked. "I'd like to know if he'd learned anything in the short time between his visit to the morgue and tending to the needs of his stomach."

"I don't know that I learned anything new, but we did come to an agreement of sorts."

Haley raised a brow. "How so?"

"I'd give him any information I learn to help him with his cases, and he returns the favor." She smiled. "Hopefully, this will give me an edge over the guys in the pit."

Haley couldn't help but wonder if the detective was playing nice because Samantha was attractive, dynamic, and single. She sipped her tea and decided a subject change was in order. "Ginger and I took a trip to Filene's. We looked in on Miss Smith, Miss St. James's dresser. She admitted to not liking Miss St. James and that the feelings were apparently mutual. And we wouldn't have gotten that much out of her if Ginger hadn't dangled a dress purchase before her."

Samantha bunched her lips. "Ginger is . . . well, I'll admit I find her intimidating."

Haley blinked back. "Really?"

"Sure. She's poised, beautiful, and well-spoken. Kinda sounds royal with that posh accent."

Haley laughed. "Those statements are all true."

"To be honest, she's not the kind of gal I'd match you with for a best friend. No offence."

"None taken," Haley said. She hadn't known Samantha for that long, but she had come to consider her a close friend. But Ginger was different. "I've known Ginger for a very long time, Sam. Since the war, actually. We met in France. I worked for the Hartigan family as a live-in nurse when her father was ailing. Ginger's been through an awful lot." Haley leaned in. "And between you, me, and the fence post, I've come to believe she worked for the British secret service."

Samantha's expression screwed up in disbelief. "As a *spy*?"

"Yes. But Ginger refuses to talk about it. She won't deny or confirm."

"Interesting," Samantha said. "Now I'm really intimidated."

Haley laughed.

"But seriously, Haley, that would make a great story."

Haley held up a finger. "No. You must not broach the subject. Believe me, I've tried. And I wouldn't want her to know we've been discussing her like this."

"Okay," Samantha said, shrinking back into her chair. "I won't. But only because I value *our* friendship. It will interest you that I had a run-in with Miss Priestley today, quite by accident."

"How small Boston sometimes feels," Haley said. "What happened?"

"I looked up Sly Hardin."

"The man who represented Miss St. James."

"And Mr. Calderwood," Samantha added, "He now represents Miss Priestley, who, by the way, is now a platinum blond."

Haley arched a brow. "Blonder than Miss St. James?"

"Much."

"Intriguing. Miss Priestley seems determined to outdo and outshine Miss St. James."

"It appears so. She stormed into his office in a self-congratulatory mood while I was there. She was Miss St. James's understudy, so naturally, she gets her part."

"So, the play isn't closing?"

"No."

"Flora Priestley is assuming Veronica St. James's role," Haley said. "If that's not motive, I don't know what is."

"Exactly my thinking," Samantha said as she set her empty teacup on the end table. "A woman could've tampered with the prop knife as easily as a man. She makes it look like her nemesis killed herself, and she gets to swoop in for the part like a buzzard. Sly Hardin wasn't too upset by losing his star client either."

"I can hardly top that," Haley said before sharing her visit to Tremont Temple Baptist Church with Ginger. "I spoke to Rees Johnson, who works as a janitor at the church as well. He only confirmed what everyone else seems to be saying, that Miss St. James was difficult to like."

"Are you going to the wedding tomorrow?" Samantha asked.

Haley nodded. "Ginger invited me, so I'll go just to spend more time with her before she leaves in two days."

"Short visit."

"She has a family to get back to."

"Mr. August wants me to cover the event for the society pages," Samantha said.

"Louisa Hartigan is almost Bostonian royalty," Haley said.

"The Hartigan family is well-known in the city." Samantha nodded. "I knew about them before I met you. Everyone who has lived in Boston for any length of time has heard about them. Which is why I'll be there, my camera as my date."

"Speaking of Boston being a small town," Haley said, "I followed Jethro Maines into a speakeasy."

"Ah, you get all the fun stuff!"

"It gets better. I believe Mr. Maines has a preference for the company of men."

Samantha stilled. "You know, I see it now. How does that change anything?"

"Maybe it doesn't," Haley said.

"The theater crowd is generally more accepting of such things."

"True, but probably not everyone. The lifestyle is illegal."

Samantha held a palm to her mouth, holding back a yawn. "Do you think Veronica St. James learned Mr. Maines's secret?"

"It's possible. If she threatened him with the information, his reputation would be ruined, as would his career."

"Blackmail?"

"I'll see if Detective Brock has checked Miss St. James's finances. Maybe there's something there." This time, Haley yawned. "We should call it a night. Tomorrow is another long day, with the wedding. It might benefit us both to take a short break from our current case." She stood and offered her hand to Samantha, helping her friend to her feet. "But from my experience with Louisa Hartigan, she is sure to make the day interesting."

CHAPTER THIRTEEN

Haley had to shake her head. Why had she agreed to come to this wedding? It wasn't like she could sit with Ginger, who was part of the bride's family, or even Samantha, who was floating about taking photographs. Instead, she sat alone, wearing the too-glamorous dress Ginger had picked out for her, without friends, family, or a date. She fanned herself with the wedding brochure, grumbling inwardly about the heat.

Exhaling, Haley gave herself a silent scolding. This day was about Louisa Hartigan and her groom. The bride looked radiant in a fitted, long-sleeved, flowing silk-and-satin gown. Lace was prominent around the neckline, and a simple veil with a jewel-encrusted pin was attached to the back of her perfectly styled hairdo. A long train hung from the back of her waist and pooled around her feet. For once, Louisa's expression wasn't a display of dramatic emotion. With her eyes on her soon-to-be husband, her gaze was peaceful, calm, and filled with certainty.

Is this what it feels like when you finally meet the one? Haley wondered if she'd ever stand at an altar, staring at another person with love in her eyes. Maybe that wasn't her lot in life anyway. Many women never married, especially since the war had created a shortage of men. Haley had her career, and that was enough for her.

"Dearly beloved," the pastor began. "We are gathered here in the presence of God, family, and friends to witness a joyous occasion, the union of Miss Louisa Hartigan and Mr. Harold Forrester."

A wave of handheld fans rustled through the following prayers. While Haley's mind wandered during the pastor's long-winded homily on matrimony, she managed to take a curious glance behind herself. Seeing an unexpected face startled her. Mr. Bertram Calderwood was in attendance. He must've arrived after she had, so she hadn't noticed him before now.

Louisa Hartigan ran in the top social circles of Boston and had mentioned she'd been a part of an exclusive group invited to a preview of the play, so in retrospect, it wasn't that surprising to see an esteemed actor there. What was a surprise was the woman beside him who couldn't keep her eyes off him, even with the spectacle of Louisa Hartigan's nuptials.

Flora Priestley and Bertram Calderwood? Haley

hadn't picked up any sense of romance between the two, but Miss Priestley's recent good fortune in becoming the leading lady to Mr. Calderwood's leading man might've changed things between them. Unless this, too, was a promotional act. Either way, Haley thought it brave of Mr. Calderwood to be seen in public, clearly in good spirits, so soon after his costar's death.

Haley caught a glimpse of Samantha, who was poised behind a pew on the other side of the aisle, her camera aimed at Mr. Calderwood and Miss Priestley. By Monday morning, their connection—whether they actually were a couple or not—would be the talk of Boston.

The vows were exchanged, and the marriage was pronounced. Haley was thankful for the short ceremony, as she expected most of the sweltering guests were. The newlywed couple marched down the aisle together, followed by the bridesmaids and groomsmen, to the foyer, where they lined up to receive and thank their guests.

Haley found Samantha, and they stood together in the receiving line.

"Wasn't that just the most beautiful wedding you've ever been to?" Samantha asked, her cheeks flushing attractively.

Haley shrugged. "I don't attend many weddings, but yes, it was lovely."

"There was only a handful of people at my wedding

when I married Seth," Samantha said wistfully. "Not much glamour to a shotgun wedding."

"I imagine it's the marriage that matters in the end," Haley said, "and not the wedding day itself."

"I missed out on both counts," Samantha said.

Haley couldn't argue that Seth Rosenbaum had been a disappointing match. "I'm sure there's a happily ever after out there for you."

Samantha squeezed Haley's arm. "For both of us."

Haley smiled stiffly. "Sure."

Bertram Calderwood stepped in line behind them, as did Flora Priestley. Her glossy, wavy blond hair was tucked under a snug-fitting turban-like hat adorned with a polka-dot ribbon and a matching side bow. Unlike Mr. Calderwood, who stared grimly at Samantha and eyed her camera narrowly, Miss Priestley gleamed like an infatuated schoolgirl.

"Miss Hawke, isn't it?" the actor said.

"It is, Mr. Calderwood," Samantha returned. "Lovely wedding, wasn't it?" Catching Flora Priestley's eye, she added, "Hello, Miss Priestley."

"I usually have to sign off on any images taken of me," Mr. Calderwood started, his eyes warming with false humility, "if the intent is to publish them in the papers."

"This is a public event, and the host and hostess have granted me permission," Samantha said coolly. "I don't need your permission."

Though Haley silently cheered Samantha on for

standing up to the actor, she didn't like the look on his face.

"It would be wise to get it, all the same," he said.

Haley stared back sharply. Had Miss St. James's murderer just delivered a thinly veiled threat to Samantha?

Thankfully, they reached the line and could both turn their backs on the man. They reached Ginger in the line, shaking her hand in turn.

"You look lovely," Samantha said.

As the sister of the bride, Ginger wore a violet silk-and-satin floor-length gown with soft sleeves. A purple satin belt tied into a bow in the back, and plenty of sparkle from her diamond necklace and earrings accessorized her outfit.

"I agree," Haley said. "Lovely. Congratulations again."

"I'm so sorry I've not had a chance to visit with you," Ginger said. "You will stick around for the reception."

Haley heard herself answer quickly. "I'm afraid I can't. I've got work waiting for me at the morgue."

"I'll be there for a short while," Samantha said, pointing to her camera.

"Very well," Ginger said, her eyes darting to the line up behind Haley, her smile dropping briefly at the sight of Mr. Calderwood. "I'll ring you tomorrow. We'll catch up."

Haley offered congratulations to the happy couple,

then slipped away, feeling a sense of freedom as she stepped outside.

Haley loved how the city slowed down on Sundays. Many folks, like Mrs. Berrymaple, went to church in the morning, where families took the time to be together. Samantha spent the whole day with Talia, enjoying simple things like going to the park and feeding the birds or playing card games on the kitchen table if the weather was poor. Then, traditionally, all of them would meet together for a relaxed evening meal—soup comprised of the week's leftovers and buns Mrs. Berrymaple would bake on Saturday afternoons.

Even criminals seemed to take a break on Sundays, at least some of them, and this looked to be like a low-crime day. With the warm spring weather, Haley thought a trip to the Charles River would be a nice calming experience to be enjoyed after the excitement of the wedding. The embankment was only a short drive from her home, west on Revere. A delightful way to spend the morning. Haley found it more satisfying to commune with God through nature.

Glistening as the morning rays bounced off the moving waters, the river was dotted with row boats and canoes manned by those seeking a more adventurous outing. The air smelled earthy and dewy, combined with the fragrance of the flora that grew along the embankment. Trees and grasses were a mix of shades of greens, and the birds that dwelt within were carefree, their birdsongs contributing to the sense of peace and tranquility.

Haley wasn't alone in her choice of Sunday destination, and many people were out enjoying the fine day with their families and loved ones. Mothers pushed prams as fathers held the small hand of an older sibling. Youths tossed a ball around, and lovers walked about hand in hand, their heads leaning in to one another. Signs of the depression weren't far off, however. Men who wore ratty clothing and were clearly unwashed could be found lying in the shade of bushes or leaning against a tree trunk.

Haley didn't mind being alone. Though she was raised with three brothers, they'd lived on a farm, so she'd had plenty of time to entertain herself, especially as the only girl. Her years in school and university hadn't given her a lot of time to be socially engaged, and as for love affairs, they tended to be short-lived and few and far between.

"Dr. Higgins!"

Haley turned toward the voice she knew very well.

"Dr. Mitchell." Haley used his formal address in turn. Gerald had been *Gerald* to her for years now, and to him, she had been simply Haley. The presence of his companion linking her arm with his was clearly responsible for the reversion. "Hello, Mrs. Cooper," Haley added politely.

"Hello, Dr. Higgins," the lady returned. "Beautiful day, isn't it?"

"Yes," Haley acknowledged. "It is."

Haley looked at Gerald, aware that he'd been staring at her. Self-consciously, she pushed wayward curls off her face.

"You seemed deep in thought," he said.

"Well, yes, there's a lot to consider."

"Any progress on the St. James case?" he asked.

"My poor nephew," Mrs. Cooper interjected. "He has the worst luck."

Hadn't Veronica St. James been the unlucky one? Haley mused. "It must be difficult for him."

"He was so put out when Bertram Calderwood was given his role," Mrs. Cooper continued. "I thought it very big of him to take a lesser role anyway."

Haley recalled Mr. House's grumblings.

"Had Miss St. James promised him the male lead in the play?" Haley asked, wondering how the actress could've convinced the producer to do so.

"She had," Mrs. Cooper said with an exaggerated nod. "They were once, uh, very friendly. I'm afraid she broke my poor Brian's heart. She hung this promise over his head like a carrot to make peace without intending to follow through. Such nonsense about her influence with the producer lady."

"Anne," Gerald said gently.

Mrs. Cooper was obviously unaware that she was supporting a motive for her nephew to have committed murder. Haley sensed the lady's nerves, maybe on suddenly meeting up with Haley herself, were causing her to be excessively chatty.

"Brian's been acting since childhood and has only dated actresses." Mrs. Cooper's eyes flashed with disapproval. "I told him it might be a good idea to search outside that pool, but no, here he goes again."

Gerald tugged on Mrs. Cooper's arm. "We must let Dr. Higgins enjoy the rest of her morning in peace." His warm gaze settled on Haley. "I know how hard she works; she deserves time to rest her mind." Tipping his hat, he added, "Good day, Dr. Higgins."

Haley watched the pair go, her chest tight with mixed emotion. She and Gerald had had their shot, and now it was time for her to really and truly let him go.

CHAPTER FOURTEEN

After a quiet Sunday, a sense of renewed vigor filled the Grove Street apartment on Monday morning. Mrs. Berrymaple prepared breakfast while everyone else dressed and got ready for their day. Samantha had the extra duty of taking Talia to school before showing up at the pit. She always arrived just a bit late and feeling frazzled, which her male colleagues found either annoying or amusing.

Johnny Milwaukee fell into the latter camp. "Hey, doll," he said. He sauntered to her desk, his fists stuffed into his pants pockets. "How's the murder story comin' along?"

Samantha blew a strand of blond hair off her face. "I was busy covering a social event on the weekend. The other story is ongoing."

"Oh, yeah, the Hartigan-Forrester shindig." Johnny

blew air out of the side of his mouth. "Weddings aren't for me."

"Weddings or marriage?"

As soon as the question left her mouth, Samantha regretted it. Johnny didn't know she knew about his wife and how she and his baby daughter had passed away. And Samantha could never tell him that she'd come across the information in an unethical way . . . she'd snooped.

"I mean, not that I care," she said weakly.

"No, it's a good question." Johnny plucked a cigarette from his cigarette case and produced a silver lighter. "You might not believe this, Sam, but I can be romantic." He lit the cigarette, sucked until the tip grew red, and released the smoke toward the ceiling. "When I want to be."

Not only did Samantha believe he could be romantic, but she wanted to be the recipient of it. However, she'd never admit to it. The rejection and humiliation that were sure to follow would be too much. Instead, she said, "I'm sure your date will be glad to hear it."

Johnny took another long draw on his cigarette. "Oh, she knows," he said, before pivoting on his heel and returning to his desk.

Samantha inserted a blank sheet of paper into her typewriter, aggressively hitting the carriage return lever as she seethed. Why did Johnny have to come to her desk all the time? She had better things to do than pine over a coworker. Besides, office romances were a bad idea. If, hypothetically speaking, a romance were to evolve between them, one of them was sure to get canned, and that someone would most likely be her.

No, there was too much at stake to let that happen. She had rent to pay, and there was Talia to think of.

She'd dropped off the film after the wedding on Saturday and had submitted the copy for the two stories, both of which were to be featured in that morning's society pages. She opened the paper, which someone had delivered to her desk, searching for her byline. She smiled when she found it.

SOCIALITE MARRIES RAILWAY TYCOON

A quick recap of the ceremony, along with some background information on the happy couple, was printed together with a photograph of them standing outside the church. Tucked in beside this story was one about the famous guest, Mr. Calderwood, and his pretty companion. Samantha thought the photo of the actor and Miss Priestley that Mr. August had selected was an interesting choice, as it'd caught the actor frowning and certainly didn't capture his usually handsome demeanor. Had the editor done that intentionally, out of spite for the ease of life handsome and rich men tended to have? Especially when it came to a ready source of pretty young women. Or had he just picked randomly, not caring?

Ultimately, it wouldn't matter to the editor, as the paper would sell regardless. But a proud man like Mr. Calderwood wouldn't like it; worse, he'd blame her.

And now that Miss Priestley had Miss St. James's role in the play, Samantha imagined she'd have to rehearse. Samantha checked her watch. Mid-morning. She wondered what time actors and actresses got out of bed and went to work.

Pushing away from her desk, Samantha grabbed her hat, gloves, and messenger bag. There was only one way to find out.

A TAXICAB STOPPED behind Haley as she parked in front of the Shubert Theatre, and Samantha stepped out.

"We're reading the same page," Samantha said when she spotted Haley waiting on the sidewalk.

Haley laughed. "So it seems."

"No Mrs. Reed today?"

"She called this morning," Haley said as Samantha stepped in beside her. "We're meeting for lunch. You should come."

"I've been away from my desk too much lately," Samantha said. "Mr. August is getting antsy. By the way, have you talked to Detective Brock lately?"

"Not since Friday." Haley cocked her head. "Why? Have you heard something?"

"No," Samantha said. "I just thought maybe you had. Are you here to see Mr. Calderwood?"

Haley nodded. "He acted strangely at the wedding, don't you think?"

"I do."

"Is he why you're here?" Haley didn't like the thought of Samantha coming to talk to a potentially dangerous man alone, though she had come to do the same thing.

"Indirectly," Samantha answered. "I thought Miss Priestley might like to comment on her new role now that she's taking over the lead."

"Yes," Haley said with a slow nod. "A nice turn of fortune for her."

The theater, naturally, was locked to the public. Haley rang the bell by the door, hoping someone inside would hear it. They didn't have to wait too long before Mr. Calderwood appeared. "Finally!" he blurted, then offered a look of apology. "Oh, I thought you were someone else."

"I'm looking for Miss Priestley," Samantha said. "Is she here?"

"I wish she were." Manners kicked in for Mr. Calderwood, and he motioned them to come inside. It had started drizzling, and both Haley and Samantha were without umbrellas.

Samantha stopped to examine her reflection in a lobby mirror, smoothing her skirt, which defined a fine figure, and patting her honey-blond hair, pinned expertly in a stylish long-bob. Despite a propensity for being in a hurry and behind the gun, Haley thought Samantha always looked put together. Looking at her own reflection, Haley couldn't help but see the contrast with the darker fabric and simpler cuts of her dress suit. She didn't even want to think about her unmanageable hair.

"Flora is being downright discourteous," Mr. Calderwood said, taking the opportunity to check his reflection as well. "Already, this lead role has gone to her head. Endless celebration of her good fortune. I wouldn't be surprised if she's still sleeping it off."

"Sleeping what off?" Haley asked innocently.

Bertram Calderwood scoffed. "Some kind of *tea*, I'm sure. I warned her against that backwoods stuff being sold on the sly—worldly-wise women such as you two know what I'm talkin' about."

"Is it like Miss Priestley to be late to rehearsal?" Samantha asked.

Mr. Calderwood shrugged. "I wouldn't bother waiting around if I were you."

"We don't mind," Haley said. "So, did you enjoy the wedding?"

The actor shrugged with a look of annoyance but didn't answer.

"You looked pretty chummy with Miss Priestley," Samantha added.

"Yeah, nice photo you printed," he said gruffly. "Ya won't get any thanks from me."

"My editor picked that one," Samantha said. "But you have to admit Miss Priestley looks good in it. The way she was staring at you."

"Ya, so?"

"Bert! Come on."

It was Brian House, who appeared in search of his fellow thespian. He narrowed his brow when he saw Haley and Samantha.

"Still waiting for Flora."

"We'll get someone else to stand in for her," Mr. House said. "We ain't got all day."

Mr. House disappeared, and Haley said, "No one seems too upset that Miss St. James is no longer around to play the part."

"Yeah, well, Ronnie made life difficult for everyone," Mr. Calderwood said. "Him especially."

"How so?" Haley asked.

"He used to be Ronnie's plaything until she tired of him. Now, if you don't mind, I gotta get back to the stage. If you see Flora on your way out," he held his thumb and forefinger a half-inch apart, "tell her she's this close to getting herself canned from the play."

Haley and Samantha stepped outside. Samantha said, "A spurned lover, huh?"

"A great motive," Haley said. "I think I'm going to drop in on Detective Brock. Do you want to come?"

Samantha looked as if she was about to say yes, then abruptly changed her mind. "You go and catch me up later. I'm going to wave down that taxi and head back to the paper."

CHAPTER FIFTEEN

As the taxi swept Samantha away, Haley caught sight of Mr. Kibble racing toward the doors of the Shubert Theatre. How serendipitous! Haley called after him. "Mr. Kibble!"

With parcels under his arms, props perhaps, the man stopped and frowned. "Hello, Dr. Higgins."

"Might I have a word?"

"I'm really very busy."

"I'll be quick, I promise."

The man never stopped walking, but he didn't ask Haley to stay away, so she stepped in beside him. "I've got a question about the knife."

"That damn knife!" Mr. Kibble seemed to pick up his pace as he stepped across the red-and-gold carpeting in the foyer. "The police are going on about that too."

He paused briefly to open the hallway door leading

to the stage. "I never messed with the knife. It worked perfectly when I put it in the drawer."

"When, exactly, did you do that?"

"Sometime in the morning, the day of the show."

"So early?"

"I have a lot of responsibilities, Dr. Higgins. I get things done as quickly as possible."

"So, there was time for someone to remove the knife, sabotage it, and put it back?"

"Certainly." They'd reached the stage, and Mr. Kibble climbed the stairs. Haley followed.

"Wouldn't that be risky, though," Haley said. "Surely some cast or crew member might've spotted the culprit?"

"One would think, but as shocking as this seems for you and that detective, the crew and I keep our heads down and do our jobs. We're not typically watching out for criminals under our noses."

Time to drop the gavel. "Mr. Kibble, did Miss St. James owe you money?"

For once, Mr. Kibble stilled. "I hardly think that's any of your concern."

"Is it the concern of the police?" Haley countered. "I could go to them and ask."

"Fine, fine." Mr. Kibble raised a palm to quiet her, then waved her into his office. He closed the door and immediately explained, "I lent her money—she always seemed short of cash—and she promised to pay it back after she was paid for doing the play. So, if you're looking for a motive from me, it's not there. Veronica was worth more to me alive than dead."

"Why was Miss St. James short of funds? It's true the reason might not implicate you, but it could shed light on someone else."

"She lost most of her fortune in the crash," Mr. Kibble said. "She tried to make it back by gambling, which it turns out she wasn't any good at. She also had an expensive lifestyle, and an image to maintain that cost a pretty penny. I should've known better, but she came to me in tears. I can be such a sucker."

"How lucky for everyone that the play will continue with Miss Priestley at the ready." Haley couldn't miss how the man's eyes lit up when she mentioned Flora Priestley. "You're fond of Miss Priestley, aren't you?" she said. "I mean, for more than the role of Evelyn Trafford?"

A crimson blush overcame his features. "Sure, what man wouldn't be?"

Roy Kibble was clearly sweet on Flora Priestley. Had his infatuation led him to do something to advance Miss Priestley's career? He mightn't have thought Veronica St. James would die from the injury.

To keep him talking, she asked, "Will Miss Priestley inherit Miss St. James's dressing room? Her personal dresser, Miss Smith?"

"The dressing room is meant for the leading lady, so yes, Miss Priestley has a right to it. She's not interested in Miss St. James's castoffs, including her dresser. Now, if you don't mind, Dr. Higgins . . ." Mr. Kibble made a show of placing his bags on his desk. "I have much to do now that the play is reopening."

Haley took his dismissal in stride and got to her feet. "Thank you for your time, Mr. Kibble. Congratulations on the continuation of your show."

Haley slid into the driver's seat of her DeSoto and checked her wristwatch. Almost noon already! Time really does fly when you're having fun. Her promised lunch meet-up with Ginger was in fifteen minutes.

Just as she engaged the ignition, Haley spotted a man exiting the Shubert Theatre. He wore his hat low over his brow, and at first, Haley couldn't make out his identity, but then, as he tried to cross the road, he turned in her direction.

Haley turned off the ignition and hopped out, hurrying along the sidewalk in her sensible pumps. "Mr. House!"

Brian House stopped just before stepping off the curb. His expression remained unchanged, lines around his eyes forming a mixed look of frustration and resignation. "Oh, hello. Dr. Higgins, was it?"

"Yes. We met in unfortunate circumstances a few days ago on opening night."

"Ronnie's demise. Not forgotten by me. Now, if you don't m—"

"I ran into your aunt yesterday. She's quite

concerned about you," Haley interrupted, not wanting to give the man a chance to dash off.

"She can be a dear thing," Mr. House said, though his voice had a hint of false concern.

"She says you and Miss St. James used to be close."

Mr. House's eyes narrowed, flashing anger. "Aunt Anne talks too much!"

Haley raised a brow at his outburst. Mr. House reined in his emotions with an inhale and a roll of his shoulders.

"That was then," he said. "We had fun for a while, sure, but that kind of thing has a shelf life, ya know. But this . . . such a shame, and now . . ."

"And now?" Haley prompted.

"We have to deal with that dumb broad, Flora," he said, and Haley noted he seemed to use the derogatory term freely with women he didn't like. He continued, "Can't even get to her first rehearsal on time. And I thought vaudeville acts were unpredictable."

Haley felt a sense of unease for Miss Priestley's well-being. "Has anyone checked in on her?"

Mr. House shrugged. "I'm not gonna do it."

"You wouldn't happen to know where she lives, would you?"

"As it happens, I did share a taxi with her once." Mr. House relayed the address. "Not a nice neighborhood, ya know what I'm saying? Not fit for a bird like Flora to live alone, and I told her so, but she just told me to mind my own business. Now, if it's all right with you,

I'm gonna get a bite to eat and probably look for a new job."

"Of course, Mr. House," Haley said. "Have a good day."

Haley returned to her DeSoto and sped along to the restaurant, hoping she beat Ginger there. Spotting her friend's glamorous stride as she moved gracefully along the sidewalk, Haley pulled up beside her along the curb.

Ginger stopped and stared. "Haley!"

Reaching over to the passenger door, Haley pulled on the handle, releasing the latch. "Get in. I'll explain on the way."

Whenever Samantha felt stumped, she'd head to the Boston Public Library. In her experience, researching the history and background of her subjects often inspired an interesting story. In this instance, her subjects were also suspects.

She exited her taxi along Dartmouth at Copley Square in Back Bay and skipped up the few stairs to the doors tucked in under a trio of archways. As she stepped inside, her senses were assaulted with a mix of smells: old books, musty shelves, and, of late, the stale stench of the unwashed as more homeless and out-of-work folk found refuge from the unpleasant realities outside.

Samantha was pleased to see that her friend Patty

Kingston, who worked as a clerk, was seated behind one of the reception desks.

"Hiya, darling," Patty said when Samantha approached. "How ya doin'?"

"Good," Samantha returned with a smile. "And you?"

"Eh. I'd rather be a kept woman, but nobody these days is gettin' what they want." She stared at Samantha with wide eyes. "Research?"

"Sorta. I'm working on the St. James story."

"Veronica St. James. What a piece of work! Though ya can't say she wasn't a drama queen."

"That she was." Samantha moved in close enough to get a whiff of the cigarette smoke that clung to Patty's hair. "Though in this case, someone else was being dramatic."

"Whatcha mean?"

"She was murdered."

Patty pulled back and slapped a palm over her mouth. "No way? Really? It's not been in the news."

"Well, if you read *The Boston Daily Record*, you'd know it has been inferred," Samantha returned. "But the police haven't made an official statement."

"So, what are you looking for?"

"Everyone involved in the play *Whispers of Deceit* is a suspect. I'm just looking for background information on them." Samantha handed Patty a small piece of paper listing the cast's names. "Just to see if anything interesting jumps out."

"Bertram Calderwood," Patty snorted. "Pretty sure you'll find a lot on him. Flora Priestley, Rees Johnson. Johnson's a very common surname, but Rees is unique. Uh, Roy Kibble, Brian House, and Sly Hardin?" She glanced up at Samantha. "The agent?"

"You've heard of him?"

"He lives on my street. A weasel, if you ask me. Used to badger me to get into acting, which maybe, nowadays, wouldn't be so bad. But believe you me, my parents taught me that acting was akin to prostitution."

"That is an old attitude," Samantha said. "I guess Hollywood films have changed people's minds on that in recent years."

It took Patty a while to dig up references to relevant magazine articles and newspaper stories. Eventually, she hauled out several large hardbound volumes filled with newspapers from previous years and put them on the reading table in front of Samantha.

Consulting Patty's references, Samantha found a plethora of tabloid-type material on Mr. Calderwood but nothing of note. She also searched for information about Mr. House and his vaudeville performances but found nothing linking him to Veronica St. James except for the current play.

Nothing was found on Flora Priestley, either. Samantha figured the young actress was too new to the scene for anyone to bother writing about her, at least up until now. She accidentally came across an article about the janitor, Rees Johnson. His unusual first name jumped out at her. Something about a brother, Dean, who'd sadly taken his life after the crash of '29. Unfortunately, this wasn't a rare tale.

Roy Kibble had been a manager at the Shubert Theatre for nearly a decade, and his name only came up in that capacity. Sly Hardin was the exception, with plenty of complaints from former clients, particularly his female clients. The discontent was primarily about unequal opportunities and wandering hands.

After meeting the man, Samantha could understand such sentiments, but it didn't point to a motive as to why the man would rig the prop knife or even how he could do such a thing without being seen by someone.

Samantha sighed with disappointment. She didn't know what she'd expected, but she'd hoped for more than nothing, which was what she had. She shouldn't have been surprised. There hadn't been anything of merit in the archives of *The Boston Daily Record* either.

"Thanks, Patty," Samantha said, while placing the documents on the desk.

"Any time, darling."

After promising to get together soon, Samantha returned to work with little to show for the day's efforts. She'd have to appease Mr. August somehow. A nice fluff piece on easy, low-cost recipes should do the trick. Mrs. Berrymaple had recently made a peanut-butter bread that called for condensed milk. Samantha knew that the paper's female readers were sure to love it.

CHAPTER SIXTEEN

On the way to Flora Priestley's apartment building, Haley relayed to Ginger the previous events of the morning. "I can't help feeling this sense of dread for the actress."

Ginger gave a reassuring nod. "One must follow one's gut in times such as these."

Flora Priestley lived in a tenement building not far from where Samantha and Talia once lived. Run-down brick buildings with little tucked-in crevices and over-flowing trash cans were, for sure, a magnet for rats. Now that the depression was in full force, places like these were overflowing with unemployed men loiter-ing. One stared at Haley and Ginger with undisguised interest which they both ignored, but the rest had glassy-eyed looks of disinterest, evidence of consistent hunger and poor nutrition.

Haley had to agree with Mr. House that this was no

place for a single young woman like Miss Priestley to live. She had a small room at the end of the hall on the second floor of the building. Haley knocked. When no one answered, she knocked again, calling, "Miss Priestley?"

Pressing her ear to the door, Haley listened for signs of life, but all she could make out was the meowing of a distressed cat.

An actual distressed cat!

Haley cast a knowing glance at Ginger who smiled as she held up a set of lock picks. "We can't let that poor animal suffer."

Ginger's speed was admirable, and in moments they heard the click of a pin giving way and the door eased open. A black cat, reminiscent of Mr. Midnight—the delightful black cat that had taken up residence at Haley's apartment—except with all four legs intact, greeted her with loud, cattish protests. They slipped inside, easing the door closed behind them.

A quick look around proved that Flora wasn't home. The studio apartment was small but tidy and sparsely furnished. A narrow bed was neatly made, and a dinner plate was dry on the rack. The cat meowed loudly, circling an empty bowl, and had clearly missed his morning meal, confirming that Flora hadn't made it home from the night before. A search through the cupboards, which proved insufficiently stocked, produced a single can of cat food. Haley opened it and placed it on the floor, finally silencing the cat's cries.

"What happened to your owner?" Haley said softly as she crouched low to pet the creature. She had a bad feeling. Flora Priestley might have been an opportunist, but she wouldn't neglect her pet. "Let's see if we can find her, huh?"

Haley took a second look around the small suite, knowing that the mind often took in the big picture at first before homing in on the details. A woolen throw hung over the foot of the bed, flowing over onto the floor.

Ginger pulled on her skirt as she squatted by the bed.

"Do you see something?" Haley asked.

Taking a pencil from the end table, Ginger dragged out a rubber sheath.

"It seems that Miss Priestley has had male company sometime in the last week."

Haley wasn't at all surprised. More women were enlightened to use birth control in these modern times, married or not, especially when an extra mouth to feed was often out of the question. "If Miss Priestley had a beau, she'd been careful not to be seen in public with him. Unless that man was Mr. Calderwood?"

Ginger got back to her feet. "Mr. Calderwood is a man and Miss Priestley an attractive woman."

"It doesn't explain why Miss Priestly failed to show up for her rehearsal," Haley said. "Where is she now? With a mystery man?"

"I fear your sense of dread might be merited,"

Ginger said. "Miss Priestley wasn't only a modern girl; she was also ambitious. Not the kind to throw away this kind of opportunity."

Haley couldn't agree more.

"I think we should go to the precinct and let Detective Brock know that Flora Priestley hadn't shown up for work and hadn't come home last night either. She could be in danger."

"You'll have to go without me, love," Ginger said. "Poor Sally's nerves are frazzled, with Louisa having gone all the way to California, and I promised her I'd return promptly after our luncheon, in hopes of soothing her."

Haley understood. They left the tenement, with its bad smells and brooding despair. After flagging down a taxi for Ginger, Haley drove in the direction of the police station.

CHAPTER SEVENTEEN

"Hello there, Dr. Higgins." Haley was well known at the police station, often having a need to confer with Detective Cluney. She took a moment to ask about him.

"From what I hear, he's having a terrific time on vacation," the desk clerk returned. "The Adirondacks or somewhat."

Haley grinned. Detective Cluney had done a good job, stringing his underlings along with his tall tale or convincing them to cover for him with the story. Haley wondered if he would be deeply offended if she walked over to the hospital to visit him. Maybe she could create a ruse, saying she saw his name on a roster, and wondered if it was the same Emmet Cluney.

"Would Detective Brock happen to be in his office?" Haley asked.

"You just caught him, Doctor," the officer said. "Breezed in just before you did."

The inference was that Haley should just head down the hall, which she did. She tapped on the open door before stepping inside. "Detective?"

Detective Brock was removing his coat and hat and glanced at Haley with a look of surprise.

"I was just thinking about you, Dr. Higgins."

"Oh?" Haley stepped inside. "What about?"

"Well, the case, naturally," he said, glancing away. "I'm not too proud to say I'm stumped. With your reputation as an amateur sleuth—"

Haley felt her eyes widen at the moniker. Is that what they called her here? *Amateur sleuth?*

"I thought maybe you could provide new insight."

"It's why I'm here," Haley said. "Miss Priestley is missing."

"Missing?" Detective Brock took a seat and motioned to the empty chair in front of his desk. "What do you mean?"

Haley lowered herself into the proffered seat. "I was in the neighborhood of the Shubert Theatre this morning—"

"The neighborhood?"

Why does the man need to interrupt? "Yes. And I thought I'd check in. I've found in the past that circling back to the scene of a crime sometimes bears fruit."

"And . . ."

"Well, the actors were there, ready to rehearse. Miss Priestley, who was Miss St. James's understudy—"

"Was she now!" the detective interjected.

"Yes, and promoted to leading lady. But she hadn't shown up."

"Maybe she spent too much time celebrating last night."

Haley raised a brow.

"Believe me, the prohibition agents are constantly up in arms about the flow of illegal hooch."

"The theory was batted around by Bertram Calderwood—" Haley said.

"He is a handsome fellow, isn't he?"

"I suppose, but the point is, Miss Priestley's absence was severely frowned upon. Mr. House inferred that the play might not go ahead, at least not in the near future."

"So, Miss Priestley frittered away her opportunity. A shame, but not a need to shoot off a flare."

"I went to her apartment," Haley said. "As a doctor, I felt concerned for her and just wanted to ensure she was all right."

The detective smiled. "I knew you were a good egg."

Haley gaped. "British slang, Detective?"

"I read," he said simply.

"Anyway, Miss Priestley wasn't in." Haley brushed over the fact that she had broken in to the woman's apartment, and emphasized the hungry cat.

Detective Brock wrinkled his nose. "I think you

might be onto something. If there's one thing I know about women, they're generally kind to animals."

It was a sweeping generalization, but in Haley's experience, it was often correct. She was about to reveal that Miss Priestley had had a man in her home when they were interrupted by a knock on the door.

Officer Bell stepped in. "G'day, Dr. Higgins," he said when he saw Haley.

"What is it, Officer?" Detective Brock asked.

"Sir, a body's been found in the Granary Burying Ground."

"That's across the street from the Tremont Temple Baptist Church," Haley said.

"Do they have an identification?" Detective Brock asked.

"Nothing on her person, sir," Officer Bell answered, "but the officer who called it in recognized her as that actress Flora Priestley."

HALEY LOVED the Granary Burying Ground. She found cemeteries, in general, to be places of calm and peace. Still, this one had the bonus of being the resting place of many important historical figures, including Samuel Adams, John Hancock, and Paul Revere. The gravestones, slim slabs of granite placed seemingly haphazardly around the yard, leaned heavily against each other as if they couldn't bear the responsibility of time.

The fact that thousands of souls were buried in this

relatively small park had a sobering effect, reminding Haley of the shortness of life and that she was well past her halfway mark.

Following the officer who met her and Detective Brock at the entrance, she dodged the tombstones, which varied greatly in size.

"This way, sir," the officer said, adding "ma'am" in Haley's direction.

The dang heat wave was persistent; Haley gave it that. She pushed damp curls off her brow, thankful she'd chosen a light-colored dress but wishing propriety would allow her to forego the stockings.

A small crowd hovered around one of the larger tombstones. Trudging carefully along the drying grass, Haley walked the distance, keeping pace with Detective Brock. A petite woman, Miss Priestley lay curled up in a fetal position behind the grave marker, her unnaturally pale hair matted against an equally pale face.

"The groundsman found her," the officer said. "At first he thought a tree bough had blown in. With her green dress, she blended in with the grass."

Detective Brock tugged on his pant legs before squatting. "Hmm. Another stabbing. I daresay this one wasn't self-inflicted."

He stood and then motioned for Haley to take a closer look. "Doctor?"

Haley, wishing she'd worn pants, pulled up a little on her skirt and leaned down. Miss Priestley's blouse had fallen open, the buttons were torn off, and a stab wound was visible over the heart, just above the rim of her brassiere. Her dress was stained a dark red where the final pump of her heart had expelled the blood. Haley tried to lift one of Miss Priestley's arms without success. "She's in full rigor mortis."

"Dead at least eight hours, then," Detective Brock said.

Haley was impressed. Most police personnel didn't keep up with forensic statistics. Even Detective Cluney, whom Haley had recited facts and figures to many times, seemed to free the information from his brain when he no longer needed it.

"Yes," Haley confirmed. "Could be longer, with the cooler overnight air slowing decomposition. A good assumption is the death occurred in the early morning hours."

"Two? Three? Four?"

Haley shrugged. "All of the above. Maybe I can get more precise on the time of death after the post-mortem. I wish I knew what Miss Priestley was doing out so late at night."

"My guess is she knew her killer," Detective Brock said. "Felt safe with him."

Haley thought that was a good guess.

The detective addressed his officer. "Has the murder weapon been found?"

"No, sir. The men search the grounds as we speak, but nothing yet."

"It seems like too much of a coincidence," Haley

started, glancing over at Detective Brock, who appeared to be staring unnervingly at her. Haley promptly returned her gaze to the body. "That both Miss Priestley and Miss St. James were acting in the same play and that within days, they were both killed with a knife or knife-like instrument."

"My thoughts exactly," Detective Brock said. "The question is, which of our suspects has something to gain by killing both of the women in the play?"

"You mean, which of our suspects might have a misogynistic bent?" The remaining cast members came to mind. Bertram Calderwood, Brian House, who liked to refer to women he disliked as "dumb broads," and Jethro Maines. None of them particularly showed esteem for the weaker sex. And she couldn't forget the stage manager, Roy Kibble.

"I think you'll have an easier time determining which ones don't," Haley said.

Detective Brock wrinkled his nose. "That's a rather cynical outlook on the males of our species, Dr. Higgins."

"When I see more men dead in my morgue at the hands of their wives or girlfriends than the other way around, I'll consider changing my mind."

"Fair enough."

"I'd pay extra attention to Mr. Kibble."

"Why's that?"

"It's possible he was in love with Miss Priestley," Haley said reluctantly. She didn't have proof, but every stone needed to be turned over. "If that was the case, he might not have enjoyed seeing her getting friendly with other men."

"I would think he would have killed Calderwood then," the detective said. "But then again, murderers aren't always logical."

The ambulance arrived, and the men came for Flora Priestley's body. "I'll meet you at the morgue," Haley said to them as they lifted the corpse onto the gurney.

"Let me know if the dead speak to you, Doctor." Detective Brock tipped his hat at Haley and walked away. As Haley watched him go, she wondered about her confused feelings about the man.

She did think of one thing. "Detective Brock?"

The man spun around, a hopeful look on his face. "Yes?"

"Someone needs to rescue Miss Priestley's cat."

CHAPTER EIGHTEEN

*H*aley arrived at the morgue just as the body was being dropped off.

Dr. Martin placed his hands on his hips and sighed. "Who do we have here?"

"Unfortunately, this is Flora Priestley."

"No, not that pretty actress from the play!"

Haley nodded grimly. "The same." She headed for her office to dispose of her hat, grateful that the morgue, insulated by the concrete basement location, was much cooler than outdoors. She asked her assistant as she walked by, "What have I missed?"

"Not too much. A slow day until now. Do you want me to prepare the body for the postmortem?"

"Yes, please, Dr. Martin." Haley didn't need approval from the mayor for this one. In his efforts to cut pennies, the mayor had asked her to cut back from any autopsies that she, or he, might deem unnecessary.

Miss Priestley's connection with one murder and being the victim of another certainly qualified her.

A few messages left on Haley's desk were written in Dr. Martin's handwriting, but there was nothing pressing that couldn't be dealt with in the morning.

Haley tied her hair off her face—a task requiring several new bobby pins, a box of which she kept in her desk—donned a clean apron, and washed her hands.

Miss Priestley's body waited for her on the porcelain table in the middle of the room, the electric light above it turned on. She cut off the clothes while Dr. Martin arranged a set of spatulas on a tray, emitting a sigh as he did so.

"Dr. Martin," Haley said, "that's the second weary sigh I've heard since I've been in. Is something on your mind?"

"Ah, Mitzie and I are on the rocks."

"I see." Haley preferred not to get involved in matters of the heart. Had her assistant had a work-related conflict or a moral dilemma, she'd have been happy to help him work that out. She hoped to change the subject by saying, "You have your work to occupy you. There's still much to learn in the forensic sciences."

"I'm not like you, Dr. Higgins, no offence. I want warm, *alive* flesh to cozy next to in the evenings."

Haley's head snapped up. She was offended. Of course she'd like someone *alive to cozy up* to, but she was also satisfied with life the way it was.

"Hand me the scalpel, Dr. Martin."

Her assistant handed the instrument to her, looking sheepish as he did so. "Doctor—"

Haley cut him off. "Dr. Martin, let's just focus on the task at hand."

All the organs were removed and weighed. Miss Priestley had been in good health. Though Haley already knew Miss Priestley had been sexually active, there was no indication that she'd had intercourse in the previous week.

Once the postmortem was completed, Haley left Dr. Martin with the task of sewing up the body and placing it in a refrigerated drawer. After washing up, she retrieved a large paper bag from the stack stored at the morgue. The bags were used mainly for depositing clothing, which usually went to the police department as evidence. As Haley picked up the soiled dress to fold and place into the bag, a slip of paper fluttered to the ground. Haley picked it up. It was blank on one side, but the other had a phone number scribbled on it in pencil. MA2332

It could have been nothing more than the number for her banker or her hair salon, or it could be a clue that would lead to the person who killed her.

Haley used the telephone on her desk, a black rotary, and dialed the operator. "Please connect me to MA2332."

Several clicks were heard on the line, the operator trying to make the connection, then finally, it started to ring. It rang uninterrupted for a couple of minutes before the operator cut in. "Appears to be nobody home, ma'am."

"Thank you. Will you please connect me to the central Boston precinct instead? To Detective Brock."

"Right away, ma'am."

This time, there was a response to the phone ringing. It was answered by the receptionist and transferred to the detective.

"Brock here."

"Detective Brock. It's Dr. Higgins. I'm calling from the morgue."

"The postmortem is completed already?"

"Yes, well, there were two of us working on this one, but I'm not calling about that."

"Oh. Dinner?"

Haley pulled the receiver from her ear and stared at it. "No," she said. Between the detective and Dr. Martin, Haley began to feel like she'd never understand men. "I've got a potential clue. Miss Priestley had a small slip of paper on her person with a phone number jotted down. I thought you might want to try tracing it."

Tracing telephone numbers back to their owners wasn't an easy task. It involved a call or a trip to the exchange office where records were kept. With so many new telephones being connected, especially in cities the size of Boston, it could take a clerk hours, if not days, to search for the number in question. The police had more pull than a layman.

"Couldn't hurt." Haley heard the shuffling of papers and what might be a search for a writing instrument. "What is it?"

Haley relayed the number.

"Anything else, Dr. Higgins?"

"I'm assuming Detective Cluney is still *on vacation?*"

Detective Brock laughed, and Haley smiled at the sound of it, warm and rhythmic.

"He is. And I'm told he's not enjoying himself one bit."

She ended the call after telling the detective that she'd let him know if she learned anything new.

"Dr. Martin," Haley said as she gathered her hat and purse. "I'm leaving for the day. I'll be late getting to the office tomorrow."

"Again?"

"Yes, again," Haley said, working to keep the annoyance out of her voice. "I'm taking Mrs. Reed to the airport."

"She's leaving Boston already, huh?" Mr. Martin said. "Had enough of us Yankees?"

Haley shook her head, leaving without replying. She was getting tired of a few certain Yankees herself.

On the main floor, she stopped to chat with the nurse on duty at the station, then asked for the room number of Emmet Cluney. Finding his room, she knocked before stepping inside. "Hello, Detective Cluney," she said with a big smile. "How's the beach?"

Detective Cluney looked like an unhappy toddler, having been sent to his bed for bad behavior. His scowl deepened when he saw her. "What the dickens? Who told you?"

"C'mon now," Haley said, taking the lone visitor chair. "Did you think for a minute I'd believe you'd gone on vacation? Without your wife?"

"You're too smart for your own good." Detective Cluney blew a raspberry. "That young upstart told ya."

"Do you mean Detective Brock?"

"Who else?"

"You don't like him?"

"I like him just fine. Just resent his youth. Damn him."

Haley laughed. "I know, how dare he be young."

"You talk like you're an old maid."

"Aren't I?"

Detective Cluney harrumphed. "Plenty of men'd be lucky to have the likes of you on their arm. If I were younger . . ."

"And unmarried," Haley added with a grin.

"What are we talkin' about here? Nonsense, when there's a murder case to solve."

Ah, Haley thought. *The real point of the detective's contention. He hates being on his back and not working.* "You're not solving it this time, I'm afraid."

"Are you?" Detective Cluney shot back. "I told Brock he'd be wise to let you in."

"And thank you for that," Haley said sincerely. "He was reticent at first but warmed up to me."

Detective Cluney smiled like the proverbial Cheshire Cat.

"What?" Haley demanded.

"I think he's sweet on you."

Haley protested. "We've only just met." She was hardly the type men got sweet on, especially at first sight. Samantha said that her luncheon with Detective Brock had been simply due to hunger. Detective Brock thought of his stomach often, with his repeated suggestion to go for dinner. Detective Cluney was out of sorts. "I take it he's been in to see you. What do you know about the murders."

"Mur*ders*? There's been more than one?"

Haley placed a fist on her hip. It really wasn't her place to present new facts to a man who wasn't officially working. "I have a feeling I'm overstepping."

"You'd better well keep overstepping."

"Another actress from the play was found this morning. I just finished with the autopsy."

"And?"

"She was stabbed just above the heart. Died quickly. Sometime last night."

"Related to the other actress's murder or coincidence?"

"It could be either," Haley admitted, "but the theory

that they're related needs to be thoroughly investigated. I'm sure it's why Detective Brock hasn't been in to see you since."

Haley didn't bother telling Detective Cluney about the phone number. She felt guilty for riling the man up when he should have been resting. And she'd stepped on Detective Brock's toes by discussing the case with the older detective before he had. She hopped to her feet.

"I should go. I just wanted to see how you're doing, which is well, by the look of things. I wouldn't be surprised if you're allowed to go home soon."

Detective Cluney lifted a stubby finger. "Not a word of this to anyone."

Haley waved to him from the door. "I'm a vault, Detective."

CHAPTER NINETEEN

Samantha had left with Talia, and Mrs. Berrymaple had hurried off to the fish market— "gotta get it when it's fresh." So Haley was home alone when the phone rang the next morning.

"Dr. Higgins," she said when she picked up the receiver.

"Good morning, Doctor. Detective Brock here."

"Oh, hello, Detective Brock." Haley braced herself for news on the case. Then again, she wouldn't doubt if an invitation to breakfast wasn't forthcoming first. She wasn't wrong.

"I'm heading to the bistro for breakfast," he said. "Care to join me?"

"I'm afraid I can't. I'm driving a friend to the airport."

"The lovely Mrs. Reed?"

"The one and the same. Do you have news?"

"I do, in fact. I thought you'd like to know we made an arrest last night."

Haley gaped, feeling the flush of sincere shock. "Who?"

"Brian House. The men swept Miss Priestley's suite and found a tie clip belonging to him. Fingerprints confirm."

Mr. House was Miss Priestley's male friend?

"The both of them certainly went to great lengths to conceal the pairing," Haley said.

"Maybe they, or he, wanted to keep their relationship from Miss St. James until after the play—or her death."

"If Mr. House had indeed been the culprit in rigging the prop knife and Miss Priestley knew it . . ."

"And the relationship went sour . . ."

"He might've killed Miss Priestley to keep her quiet . . . Oh."

"Oh what?"

"I ran into his aunt on Sunday. She inferred Mr. House had been dating another actress." Haley chastised herself. She might've saved Miss Priestley's life if she'd put the dots together sooner.

"Actresses are a dime a dozen," Detective Brock said intuitively. "There would be no way you could've guessed which one."

Haley felt a warm surge of appreciation for the detective's sensitivity. For the briefest moment, she regretted being too busy to meet him for breakfast.

"Has he confessed?" she asked.

"No. Quite the contrary. Vehemently denies it and is heartily threatening to sue the department."

"He does seem to have a dynamic range of emotions," Haley said. So unlike his soft-spoken, if loquacious, aunt. "I suppose that's an asset for an actor."

"House admits to wanting the lead role and that Miss St. James had promised to convince Mrs. Meadows to give it to him."

"I wonder if she even asked the producer at all," Haley said. "And if Mr. House discovered this, I imagine it would have made him very angry. I suppose this rules out Mr. Kibble. I really thought he might be a candidate."

"I checked him out too. Has an alibi for the time of Miss Priestley's death. His sickly mother lives in Waverley. He'd gone to check in on her. The neighbors confirm."

"Good to know." Haley let out a breath. Maybe it was over, and justice would be meted out.

"Give my regards to your friend," Detective Brock said, ending the conversation.

"Thank you for calling," Haley said.

"My pleasure."

Haley could hear the smile in his voice as he contin-ued. "Cluney was right about you. We need to be on the same team, but I could've used a warning that you'd gone to see the old guy."

"Sorry about that," Haley said, feeling a smile cross her face as well. "I hope he wasn't too hard on you."

"The nurses had to break up a wrestling match on the hospital bed, but I wasn't hurt too badly."

Haley laughed.

"Goodbye, Dr. Higgins."

"Goodbye."

Haley chuckled, then checked her wristwatch for the time. Her heart stammered. She was going to be late picking up Ginger. But first, she had to make another call. Thankfully, Samantha picked up right away.

HALEY RAN up the steps to the Hartigan brownstone, and a maid answered her knock. Ginger hovered behind her.

"So sorry I'm late," Haley said. "Got a call just as I was leaving."

Ginger, wearing a suitable travelling ensemble of a summer suit, low-heeled shoes, and a side-brimmed hat, looked at Haley, her green eyes wide with concern.

"Nothing serious, I hope."

"I'll tell you all about it in the car."

"Very good," Ginger said. "We can go. I've already said my goodbyes to Sally."

A footman carried Ginger's luggage to the car and fit it into the backseat. The Ginger Haley knew would've had so much luggage her DeSoto wouldn't have managed to hold it all, but that was when travel by steamship was days long. With air travel becoming an accessible and convenient way to make the journey, time was saved at the expense of too much baggage.

"I can't believe you're leaving already," Haley said once they were heading toward the ferry that carried passengers to East Boston. "I feel like I barely got a chance to see you."

"I feel the same way." Ginger released a long breath. "Louisa's wedding took far too much of my time, but at least we did get to spend a couple of lovely days together."

"Working a murder case."

"And wasn't it fun!" Ginger said. "I only wish I could be here when you solve it. I will raise a glass of quality brandy in your honor. Though," her expression sobered. "I'm dreadfully sorry to hear about Miss Priestly's demise."

"As am I," Haley returned. "However, an arrest was made last night."

"Oh? Who?"

"Brian House."

Haley caught Ginger's green eyes rolling upward as she contemplated the news. "You don't think it's him, do you?"

"I really can't say."

Ginger's accent on the word "can't" sounded very British to Haley, and she mused about how her friend had really made England her home.

"He'll get a fair trial, either way," Haley said. "If it wasn't him, then we'll find it out."

Ginger giggled. "*We* will?"

"You're not the only one with an in at the police department, Ginger," Haley said lightly. "I'm just not married to one of them." Changing the subject, she asked, "Have you heard from Louisa? I gather they made it safely to their honeymoon destination."

"California!" Ginger waved white-gloved hands in exasperation. "Louisa was wise to keep her intentions from her mother until the last possible moment. Sally was not happy."

"What does she have against California?" Haley asked. "I've heard it's a nice state, with dryer, warmer weather."

"That's what Sally has against it. She's afraid it will lure her daughter and new son-in-law away from Boston. I tried to reassure her that Louisa was a Bostonian through and through and would never leave."

It was a pleasant ferry ride across the harbor to East Boston, where the small airport was located. Haley and Ginger stood on the passenger deck facing sunny skies, enjoying the warm breeze, but thankfully a cooler one than the week before. It was a short journey, and soon, they were back in the DeSoto and driving into the Boston Airport parking lot.

After parking, Haley went in search of a porter.

Though Ginger had to travel with less to fly, she still had more than she could carry on her own.

"Oh, here," Ginger said, handing Haley a linen bag. "Louisa gave me a bunch of magazines, *Boston Life*, that she'd collected over the years. I browsed through them and found a few that featured Miss St. James. I thought you might like to see them."

"Yes," Haley said. "That could be interesting. Thank you."

Ginger pouted attractively. "I do hate goodbyes, especially when I don't know how long our time apart will be."

"I hate them too," Haley said. "But we'll keep writing."

"And now that I've met the people in your life, I can put faces to names. Samantha is delightful. I do regret not having a chance to say goodbye in person."

"I'll do it for you. Oh, Ginger!" Haley held out her arms. "I will miss you."

Ginger accepted Haley's embrace. "And I you."

"Give Basil, Scout, and Rosa my love," she said.

"I will."

Haley swallowed back sadness as she watched Ginger walk away. Before disappearing through the waiting room door, Ginger turned and waved. Haley waved back and whispered. "Until we meet again, my friend."

CHAPTER TWENTY

Samantha had to admit that sharing living quarters with the city's medical examiner had its perks. She was the first to get the story about Flora Priestley's death. Sadly, a body found in a cemetery wasn't considered news—many hobos and down-and-outers used the grounds to end their lives. It was why journalists hadn't arrived en masse to cover the story; all of them, including Samantha herself, were rueful when they found out it had been an actress.

Samantha had delivered the story to Mr. August as soon as she heard about it from Haley, and she was tickled to read it in the morning paper. Seeing her name, Sam Hawke, in the byline would never get old. However, the fellows in the pit weren't exactly congratulatory. Samantha kept her gaze averted, purposing to ignore the jibes, but it was impossible to block them out.

"Must be nice to be in the back pocket of power."

"She's cutting in line."

"Unfair advantage," Doug Wallenburg mumbled after blowing a billow of smoke toward the nicotine-yellow ceiling.

"Yeah, maybe I should start sleeping with the medical examiner," Fred added.

Samantha glared at the man. What did he care? He was a *sportswriter*. "That is crude and uncalled for, Mr. Hall. I won't have you slandering Dr. Higgins' good name in that manner."

In a slow and meandering fashion, in the same way he seemed to approach life, Johnny Milwaukee said, "Cut it out, fellas." He straightened his long black tie, adjusting the knot as he continued, "You can't deny that you don't have a guy who gives you tips. Wally, you got a call, didn't you? I saw you pick up your phone. Same as me. Just didn't bother going."

Samantha gave Johnny a small smile of thanks. She was grateful that he'd come to her defense but hated that she needed defending in the first place. She returned her focus to the lady's piece on sprucing up the home with wildflowers, a low-cost alternative to purchasing cut stem varieties from stores. *Purple columbines sharing a vase with the red swamp milkweed add a vibrant and contrasting splash of color!*

All the while, the case at hand continued simmering in the back of her mind. Why were both Veronica St. James and Flora Priestley dead? Was it at the hand of a man who resented successful women such as Miss St. James, or women poised to take the lead, as in Miss Priestley?

Samantha was glad she'd agreed to meet Haley for lunch after she returned from dropping Mrs. Reed off at the airport. Two heads were better than one.

She was wrapping up the floral piece—*Nothing like a bunch of yellow buttercups to brighten up your day*—when, in her peripheral vision, she saw Johnny answer the telephone on his desk. *Is that a new lead?* Officer Bell sometimes told her when a crime of interest occurred, but he hadn't called her about Flora Priestley. She and Tom Bell had almost been a couple once, but she'd put the brakes on. Now he'd found a new gal and married her. Samantha supposed she'd need to look for a new police contact, which was depressing. It wasn't easy to make that kind of alliance, at least without certain strings being attached.

Samantha surreptitiously watched Johnny's face for clues—a frown or buckling forehead, a rapid scribbling of notes on his notepad—but what she saw was a smile, the kind that formed when you were thinking of something pleasant. *Or someone.*

She heard him say, "I'll meet you there," before hanging up. He grabbed his coat and hat and headed past Samantha's desk toward the door. Samantha made a show of looking particularly lost in thought, riveted to her typewriter.

Drat the man. What do I care, anyway? I liked him, sure,

as a person and a coworker. Nothing more. No, no, no, nothing more than that. She cupped her forehead with a palm and sighed.

"Everything all right, Miss Hawke?"

Samantha straightened as she turned toward the soft, kind voice of Max Owen, the young, shy photographer.

"Yes, sure." She was rescued from further scrutiny by the ringing of her phone. Max nodded before continuing on his way toward the darkroom. Now, there was a nice fellow. Too bad he was so young. And too quiet for Samantha's liking, but he'd make some young lady very happy once he found the confidence to speak to one.

She picked up her receiver and spoke, "Sam Hawke here."

"Hi Sam, it's Haley."

"Are you canceling our lunch date?" Samantha said. "Has something happened?"

"I'm not canceling lunch, and yes, something has happened. Brian House has been arrested for the murders of Miss St. James and Miss Priestley."

Samantha's focus darted around the room. None of the other reporters were getting calls, but they probably would be soon enough. Samantha scribbled down all the information Haley had to offer.

"Thanks, Haley. I owe you. See you soon."

Samantha quickly typed up the story, nearly finishing by the time the other phones in the room started ringing. Poor Johnny was too busy wooing his new squeeze to get a chance on the story. Didn't matter. Samantha had the scoop. She tugged on the paper, releasing it from the typewriter, then with shoulders back and the confidence of a seasoned reporter, she delivered her story to Mr. August.

"You certainly have your finger on the pulse on what's happening in the city, Miss Hawke." Mr. August grabbed his red pencil and made notations as he read. "Make these changes, then take it down to composing."

Fred Hall muttered under his breath. "Vixen. Leave something for the men, will ya?"

Samantha ignored the obnoxious man, rewrote the story to Mr. August's specification, and then took the work downstairs to the basement where the composing room was located.

Inky, the head composer, was a mole-like man with ink-stained fingers. "You're goin' to wear a path in the steps with those heels at the rate you're goin', miss." He chuckled.

Samantha was just glad to have the work and the accompanying paycheck to buy shoes, should she need to. "Just make sure it makes this afternoon's edition, Inky," she said kindly. "Mr. August's orders."

Back at her desk, Samantha removed a small mirror and a tube of lipstick from her purse. She always felt better after applying color to her lips. She turned her back to the men in the room, giving her lips a good layer of mandarin-orange.

Samantha pinned a small hat to her head at the fashionable angle and donned the lace gloves she'd chosen that morning. She was meeting Haley at a nearby cafe since Haley had a car and she didn't. Even so, the short walk caused her to break into a sheen. She was patting her forehead with a handkerchief when she saw Johnny walking on the other side of the road, his hands in his pockets, his cap low. He was shuffling along with his typical carefree gait. Samantha's heart pinged at the sight of him, then crushed when she noticed the lady walking beside him, laughing at something he said. It was the same woman Johnny had taken to the Shubert Theatre.

Samantha inhaled deeply. Never mind Johnny and his gal. She had work to do. Samantha owed Haley lunch and was glad her friend was already at the bistro, waiting. Samantha would put Johnny out of her mind, at least for an hour.

CHAPTER TWENTY-ONE

The cafe was half empty. *A sign of the times,* Samantha thought, *with more people pinching pennies and eating at home.* She spotted Haley sitting at a table along the wall and took a chair opposite her. "How did it go with the drop-off?"

Haley grinned. "Well, since *I* was driving, it was fine."

Samantha wrinkled her brow in confusion. "I don't understand."

"Ginger is excellent at many things, but driving isn't one of them." Haley's eyes moved upward, softening as if she remembered something fondly. "It was hard to see her go. She told me to say goodbye to you for her."

"I'm glad I got to meet her," Samantha said sincerely. Ginger Gold had become a mythical legend to her, and finally meeting her had made her real and human.

They ordered sandwiches and coffee. The coffee came soon after, and as Samantha stirred in a bit of sugar, she said, "Thanks again for the tip, Haley. You're better than any contact on the police."

"I know someone's going to get the story. Might as well be you."

"I just can't believe they got him already." Samantha shook her head. "It makes sense when you think about it. Unrequited love, broken promises, betrayal, and a man like Mr. House with barely controlled rage." Samantha snapped her fingers.

"Seems very plausible," Haley said.

Their lunch arrived, and after a bite of her cucumber and chive sandwich, Samantha nodded to the pile of *Boston Life* magazines sitting on one side of the table.

"Ginger gave these to me," Haley said after a sip of coffee. "Her sister didn't want them anymore."

Samantha laughed. "She thought *you*'d want them? No offence, but they're just a collection of the type of socialite and ladies' interest pieces I write."

"I read the stuff *you* write," Haley said, lifting her sandwich to her mouth. "And I don't mind admitting I've learned a few things."

"Oh?" Samantha said with a sparkle of curiosity in her eyes. "Like what?"

"Like, um, makeup advice and fashion trends. Just because I don't jump on every bandwagon doesn't mean I don't want to know that bandwagons exist."

"I stand corrected," Samantha said, glancing again at the pile. "I'm assuming you found something of interest in those magazines."

"Ginger pointed out that Veronica St. James was frequently featured, especially in the mid-twenties." Haley had earmarked a few pages. "Take a look."

Samantha hovered over one image, narrowing her eyes.

"What is it?" Haley asked.

"This man that Miss St. James is with looks familiar." She turned the magazine around so Haley could see. Samantha continued, "He's identified as Dean Johnson."

Haley stared at the man in the image, then glanced at Samantha. "He looks a bit like Rees Johnson. Brothers?"

"I did a bit of digging at the library. Rees Johnson had a brother named Dean."

"Had?" Haley asked. "Is he deceased?"

"Took his own life after the crash."

Haley hummed. "Not a unique story, but, interestingly, Rees Johnson and Miss St. James knew each other, or at least knew of each other, aside from crossing paths in the theater in *Whispers of Deceit*." She lowered the crust of her sandwich to her plate. "Wait a minute."

"What?" Samantha asked.

"I just remembered something Bertram Calderwood said. That, on one occasion early in their relationship, Miss St. James wouldn't stop talking about a guy named Dean."

"Could it be the same Dean? Dean Johnson?"

Haley leaned back in her chair. "Maybe we should have a talk with Mr. Johnson about his brother."

IT WAS quiet at Tremont Temple Baptist, especially after the recent wedding celebration. The sanctuary had been cleaned up, with little evidence of the crowd that had recently filled the place remaining. Haley wondered if Rees Johnson had been solely responsible for returning things into proper, holy order or if he had had help. A quick scan of the church produced no sign of the man.

They found a jolly-looking lady with thick round glasses in the church office.

"Oh, hello," she said cheerily. "I'm afraid the pastor's not in. I'm Miss Pollymore. Can I help you?"

"I'm Dr. Higgins, Boston's chief medical examiner, and this is Miss Hawke." Haley purposefully omitted Samantha's job description as many people were prone to clam up around reporters.

"The lady doctor!" Miss Pollymore's gray brows jumped. "I heard about you. In the papers! So brave of you."

Haley wasn't sure what part of her career choice made her brave, but she accepted it as a compliment.

"We're looking for Mr. Rees Johnson, a janitor here," she said.

"Oh, yes." Miss Pollymore shook her head. "Mr. Johnson, poor man."

"Why do you say that?" Haley asked. "Is he unwell?"

"See, I'm not one to gossip." Miss Pollymore pushed up on her glasses. "But I do worry about the man. He's always down in the dumps, except when he got that extra job in that theater. That cheered him, but I don't see that working in such a place is suitable for a Christian man, but who am I to judge? And then . . ."

"And then the star of that play was killed," Samantha said, finishing for her.

"Yes. So tragic, even if she was an actress. And it's the second time poor Mr. Johnson has lost someone close to him."

"In what way were Mr. Johnson and Miss St. James close?" Haley asked.

"Oh, well, that actress was once close to Mr. Johnson's brother. Really close. Some said they were engaged, but then he lost his money in the crash, and well, he died. Poor Mr. Johnson. No wonder he's so ornery now."

"What do you mean?" Haley asked.

"Yesterday, he had a spat with a young woman right here in the lobby. Made her cry. He stormed out after and hasn't come back since."

"What did the young woman look like?"

"Blue eyes." She made a face. "And very, very blond hair, unnaturally so."

Haley shared a look with Samantha. *Flora Priestley.*

"Didn't hurt her looks much, but so *worldly*," Miss Pollymore continued. "And wait until she gets older."

"Would you happen to have an address for Mr. Johnson?" Haley asked. "We'd like to send him our condolences."

Miss Pollymore wrote out an address and handed it to Haley. They thanked the receptionist and then conferred outside on the sidewalk.

"For some reason, Flora Priestley came here to see Rees Johnson," Samantha said, holding out her hand for the slip of paper with the address on it.

"They argued," Haley handed the paper over. "Did she confront him about something?"

Samantha handed the paper back. "Accuse him of murder?"

Haley let out a long breath. "It could be why she's dead now."

Haley returned to the morgue, leaving Samantha to catch a taxi back to the paper. She wanted to call Detective Brock to let him know what they'd just learned. Chances were, he had already talked to the church receptionist, but it wouldn't hurt to make sure.

She pushed away the niggling thought that it would be a good excuse to speak to him again.

Dr. Martin greeted her in his usual amiable way, and Haley wondered if he'd already recovered from losing his girlfriend. Some people were good at bouncing back.

"Slow day," he said. "A heart attack, but no request for an autopsy. I already tagged him and prepared him to be sent to the undertakers."

"Very good," Haley said. "Any messages for me?"

Dr. Martin shook his head. "Like I said. Slow day."

Haley stepped into her office and sat at her desk. The slip of paper she'd found on Flora Priestley's person was still there, lying on the top of her desk from when she'd called it in to Detective Brock. She wondered if he'd been able to trace the number. She picked up the receiver and dialed the operator, expecting the connection to ring unanswered as it had the first time, but was surprised by a gruff, masculine "Hello?"

"Oh, hello," Haley said quickly. "Is Mr. Rees Johnson there?" It was a wild guess, but seeing that Rees Johnson might've been the last person to see Flora Priestley alive, she gave it a shot.

And was rewarded.

"Who's asking?"

"This is Dr. Higgins," Haley said. And then the call was lost, and a dial tone rang in her ear. She stared at the receiver. Had Rees Johnson just hung up on her?

Something told Haley that they needed to hurry, that Rees Johnson might run out of town. She called the police precinct but was disappointed that Detective Brock wasn't in. She relayed Rees Johnson's home address.

"Someone needs to check in on him. I think he's responsible for two deaths. No, I don't have proof. Just make sure Detective Brock gets this message."

THE FIRST THING Samantha did when she returned to the paper was disappear into the archives room, where she found a significant number of hardcover volumes of the newspaper bound into books, sorted month by month and year by year. She was interested in any story that had ever been printed about Veronica St. James, no matter how far back.

Max Owen walked in and stuttered to a stop when he saw Samantha. He was about to leave when Samantha spoke.

"Mr. Owen. Please don't leave on my account."

Max dipped his chin. "All right, Miss Hawke. I'm just looking for something for Mr. Milwaukee."

"Mr. Milwaukee doesn't like to do his own dirty work, does he?" Samantha could hear the bitterness in her voice. She softened it and added, "He's lucky to have a friend in you."

Max nodded and pulled open a file cabinet. "He's lucky to have a friend in you, too, Miss Hawke."

Samantha didn't think she and Johnny were friends.

Friendly, yes, but not friends. "I think he has a new friend now. Do you know her name?"

"Oh, you must mean Miss Jean Evans."

"Oh."

Max stopped what he was doing and faced her. "I hope I'm not speaking out of line, but I think you should know that Mr. Milwaukee has strong feelings for you."

"Strong feelings?"

Max blushed. "You know. Of the romantic kind."

Samantha laughed. "He has a funny way of showing it."

"He's just scared, Miss Hawke. And don't tell him I said that. It's just he's the kind who doesn't like to take chances with his heart."

Samantha looked away, worried the shame could be seen on her face. She knew why Johnny was protecting his heart, and she had no right to know. "Well," she finally said, swallowing, "maybe it's for the best, left as it is."

"Yes, ma'am." Max offered a weak smile, then left.

Samantha wasn't sure how she felt about Max's revelation. Was it true that Johnny had pulled away, not because he cared less about her, but because he cared more?

She shook it off. Right now, she had to focus on the matter at hand. Her eyes settled on a story written in November 1929 with the scandalous headline: ST.

JAMES BREAKS ENGAGEMENT AFTER FIANCÉ LOSES BIG IN CRASH.

Fiancé? Why hadn't Rees Johnson ever mentioned that Veronica St. James and his brother had once been engaged? Seemed like a big deal.

Also, a big motive.

Veronica had also lost money. The next story about her concerned her new relationship with the up-and-coming Bertram Calderwood, but from what Samantha had seen, Mr. Calderwood wasn't interested in Miss St. James romantically—a weak motive to kill her.

Samantha jumped to her feet and ran to her desk in the pit.

Johnny glanced up from his typewriter, frowned, and said, "Where's the fire, doll?"

Samantha didn't have time to banter. She picked up her phone and dialed the operator, connecting to the morgue. It seemed like ages before Dr. Martin answered.

"Sorry, Miss Hawke. The doc is out."

"Did she say where she was going?"

"She left in a hurry. Something about John?"

"Johnson. Thank you."

"Do you need help, Sam?" Johnny was at her desk, a look of concern on his face.

"I'm not sure. It could be nothing, but I think Haley might be in trouble."

"We can take my roadster. Where to?"

Samantha relayed Rees Johnson's address, hoping that they'd find out nothing more than that they'd wasted time on a wild goose chase.

HAVING LIVED in the city for many years, Haley knew central Boston like the palm of her hand. If the traffic wasn't too heavy—it'd gotten worse in the last few years with motorcars overtaking horses and horse-drawn carts and buggies, even in these depressed days—she could make it to any address within ten minutes. Even so, Haley's heart beat with the worry that she would be too late, that she'd find Rees Johnson's apartment vacated, him having escaped Boston and the hands of the police. She found a spot to park a half block away and walked swiftly along the sidewalk.

"Haley!"

Haley stopped short, then pivoted toward the familiar voice. "Samantha?" She stared at Sam, taking in Mr. Milwaukee, who stood beside her. She became increasingly aware of other pedestrians stopping. "What are you doing here?"

Samantha grabbed Haley's elbow and then pointed up. "It's Rees Johnson. He's standing on the ledge!"

Haley's breath hitched as she saw a man on the rooftop of a six-story redbrick building, balancing precariously on the edge. Even from that distance, Haley could see that Mr. Johnson's clothes were wrinkled and hung loose, as if he'd spent a sleepless night wearing them; his face was a cloud of darkness.

Without thinking twice, Haley sprinted away.

"Haley!"

"I can't let him jump!"

Haley had always been grateful that she was athletic, even if that wasn't a trait admired in women, but it helped her get quickly to the roof, taking two steps at a time.

"Mr. Johnson?" she called out, panting as she burst out of the door that gave onto the flat roof of the building.

"Stay away!"

"It's Dr. Higgins, chief medical examiner for the city of Boston."

"I know who you are, damnit. I haven't lost my memory."

"Please step away from the edge, Mr. Johnson."

"Why? They're just going to throw me in jail and put me in the electric chair anyway."

"I believe, deep down, you're a just man, Mr. Johnson."

"If you believe life is just, you're a fool, Doctor. And I'm a bigger fool than all of them."

Rees Johnson swung an arm around, nearly losing his balance. The crowd gathered below let out a loud "ahh," and Haley gasped with them. She had a strong stomach, as a person must to work in her profession, but she didn't relish the idea of seeing a man fall to his death and the subsequent physical consequences. Her mind raced for a way to calm the man, but the fact was, he was right. His plight would be simpler if he let himself fall. Justice would entail a lengthy time in jail, followed by a notorious trial, which, based on overwhelming evidence, would end in his conviction.

Below, she could see Samantha and Mr. Milwaukee, him with a camera at the ready and pointing high. Another figure approached, and from his lanky gait and dented fedora, Haley recognized him as Detective Brock. Samantha pointed, and the detective looked up.

"Mr. Johnson," Haley said sharply, not wanting the man to see the police heading into the building. "How long have you lived here?"

"W-what?"

"How long have you lived in this building?"

"I dunno. Ten, fifteen years. What does it matter now?"

"Do you have next of kin? I'm assuming you have your financial matters in order."

Mr. Johnson shot Haley a look. "It was just me and my brother. And now I don't have him because of that . . . that . . . Veronica. I told him to watch her—I don't trust those Hollywood types—but she had him in a spell. Now I have nothin' and no one.'"

Keep him talking.

"It's true that Miss St. James gave your brother bad advice. A lot of people lost money in the crash. I'm sorry."

"Sorry for what? Did you lose too?"

"Not money, no. But like you, I lost a brother."

"You're just saying that to keep me from jumping. I tell ya, it ain't gonna work."

"It's true. My brother Joe was murdered."

Rees Johnson's expression crumpled. "I miss him so much."

"I know, but it gets a bit easier, Mr. Johnson. With time."

"I don't got no more time."

"You still have some time," Haley said. "On this earth. You can't change what you've done, but you could right other wrongs."

Mr. Johnson's eyes, glassy with pain, held Haley's gaze. "I'm guilty of murder. The Bible says if you hate someone in your heart, it's the same as being a murderer, and I hated Veronica."

Something skipped in Haley's mind. Mr. Johnson pushed out his quivering bottom lip.

"What did you and Miss Priestley fight about?"

Mr. Johnson stilled, squinted. "What?"

"The church secretary, Miss Pollymore, said she saw the two of you arguing."

"Miss Pollymore is a gossip of the worst kind." For a moment, Mr. Johnson seemed to forget about the fact he was standing on the ledge of a building. "Those types love front-of-the-church jobs, all the better to wag their tongues."

From the corner of her eye, Haley saw the door to

the roof crack open, and Detective Brock's crooked fedora poked through.

"So you and Miss Priestley weren't fighting?" Haley asked.

"Well, sure, but it didn't have anything to do with the play or Veronica dying."

Haley made sure to hold Mr. Johnson's eye, careful not to give away that they were no longer alone on the rooftop. "What did it have to do with?"

"Why don't you ask her?"

Because she's dead?

"Why don't you just tell me," Haley urged.

"She saw someone fiddle with the prop knife." Mr. Johnson inhaled sharply. "I told her to go to the police, but she wouldn't."

"Who did she see?"

"She wouldn't tell me. Said the information would come in handy in the future. Can you believe it? I told her she was being careless and selfish. That made her mad. She told me I'd better watch my back." He stared down at the crowd below. "As if that'll matter now."

Haley spoke quickly, hoping to stop him from falling forward. "Was that the last time you saw Miss Priestley?"

Before he could answer, Detective Brock wrapped his long arms around Mr. Johnson's torso and tugged him onto the roof.

"Hey!" the man protested, his arms flailing, his voice like a wild animal caught in a snare. "No!"

Detective Brock had his cuffs on the man before he could wrestle free. "Rees Johnson, you're under arrest for the murders of Miss Veronica St. James and Miss Flora Priestley." He handed the cuffed man to the two officers who'd come out onto the roof after him. "Take him to the station," Detective Brock said. "I'll be there shortly."

Haley took a moment to run a hand over her outfit, push curls off her face, and pat at her hair, tightening some of the pins. When she felt put back together, she looked at Detective Brock, who was staring at her with amusement.

"I see you got my message," she said, folding her arms over her chest.

"Are you sure you're in the right profession?" The detective smiled. "Seems to me you do well in police work."

"Yes, well, it's hard enough for a woman to gain respect in medicine, though the ages-long tradition of female nursing helps. Police work is far less hospitable."

"A shame that is, too. Dinner?"

"What?" Haley didn't know if she'd ever get used to this man's sudden subject change.

"Are you hungry? It's almost dinner time."

"I suppose I could eat," Haley said with a slight reluctance as she approached the rooftop door. The scene she had just witnessed had left her shaken.

Detective Brock stepped in beside her, hurrying to

the door before she reached it, holding it open. "I know this great Italian place."

"Please, Detective. You're new to town. I've lived in Boston most of my life. Nothing is new to me."

"I stand corrected. Could you recommend a good Italian place?"

"I could," Haley said, giving a slight smile in spite of herself. "But to be clear, this isn't a date."

"Of course not." Detective Brock motioned for her to take the stairs down ahead of him. "Ladies first."

As Haley headed down the stairs, it wasn't with the usual sense of satisfaction she felt when a case was solved. A man was going to his execution, and it didn't feel right.

CHAPTER TWENTY-TWO

Three weeks after the arrest of Rees Johnson
—who'd become catatonic, neither admitting nor denying the murders—Haley was busy at the
morgue, finishing up paperwork. The play, *Whispers of
Deceit*, hadn't recovered from the death of two of its
stars, and a new play was opening that week, keeping
Mr. Kibble ecstatically busy. Haley had heard from
Samantha, who was covering Bertram Calderwood's
career and love life, that the famous actor was filming a
talkie in California.

Brian House had gone back to vaudeville after
having moved to New York. This piece of news she'd
heard after bumping into Gerald, who updated her on
Mrs. Anne Cooper's nephew. He and Anne were doing
well and enjoying each other's company, he'd said, and
Haley was happy for him. Sincerely, this time.

As for Haley's love life, there wasn't one. She kept

busy with her work, helping Samantha occasionally with caring for Talia—a dear girl, in Haley's estimation —and a round of golf on the links when the time and weather merited it.

Mrs. Meadows had died. Haley hadn't considered the producer since the case closed, as she hadn't had the privilege of meeting her. Samantha had been thoroughly impressed with the older woman, and readied herself to attend the funeral.

Samantha walked into the kitchen, somehow looking as fashionable as the ladies she wrote about despite being dressed entirely in black. "Haley, why don't you come with me?"

"I never even knew the woman."

"But think about how you enjoy a good funeral; this one promises to be all that and more. I've heard her granddaughter is inheriting everything! Besides, I don't want to go by myself. It's tacky."

Haley held in a grin. She had to admit she found funerals morbidly interesting, and this one was tied to two murders. "All right," she said. "But don't expect me to sing along with the hymns. I don't have the voice for it."

Quite coincidentally—and Haley was beginning to feel there were too many of those—the funeral was held at Tremont Temple Baptist Church, and Haley couldn't help but note the difference in atmosphere from the last time she'd been seated in the sanctuary for Louisa Hartigan's wedding. Instead of flashy colors, the attendees were a sea of black, frowns replaced smiles, and the music was a suitable dirge rather than the upbeat bridal march.

What the two events had in common was a plethora of flowers, and Haley no longer felt bad that she'd been remiss in not sending some.

The casket was opened for viewing in a side room, and Haley and Samantha stepped in line, which crawled slowly by the body.

"She looks exactly like she did when I met her," Samantha whispered. "She didn't seem ill at all, then. A lot of vim and vigor that I admired and could only hope I possessed at her age. Looking at her, I'd swear she was only sleeping."

Haley whispered back, "Mr. Oakley did a good job."

"Who?"

"The undertaker who did the embalming."

"And I thought you had an odd job."

They shuffled along and, as those in front of them did, returned to the sanctuary where they were seated.

As the guests filed in, Haley took note of those she recognized. Mr. Kibble, his knees jumping with his inability to sit still, sat with a group of fellow theater crew and others who had benefited from Mrs. Meadows's unique hands-off style.

"Mr. Calderwood's dresser, Mr. Birnberg, is here with his wife," Haley said. The dresser had been ruled out as a suspect as it had been proven he was with his wife all day and had made that trip to the corner store and purchased sleeping draught. "Interestingly, no sign of Miss St. James's dresser, Miss Smith."

The organist started a new, dramatic dirge, signaling the start of the funeral. Pallbearers carried the closed casket down the aisle as a few mourners from the family walked along behind, one of whom made Haley sit up.

"Isn't *that* Miss Lara Smith, Veronica St. James's dresser?" she whispered in Samantha's ear.

"It sure looks like her." Samantha worked her lips. "Don't tell me Miss Smith is the granddaughter?"

"How strange it hadn't come up?" Haley returned. Strange and unsettlingly convenient.

The pastor led the congregation in an opening prayer before beginning the eulogy, a comforting sermon on the promise of a glorious afterlife for believers, followed by a couple of appropriate hymns and a prayer sending the departed into the arms of God. Everyone in the room recited the Lord's Prayer, and the ceremony ended with the pastor giving a prayer of blessing.

The pallbearers then picked up the casket, taking it back down the aisle toward the door where a hearse would be waiting to deliver it to the cemetery for the interment.

Miss Smith and the other mourners—who turned out to be longtime employees of Mrs. Meadows—greeted those who'd come to offer their last respects.

Haley and Samantha waited until they were nearly

the last in line. Miss Smith, who'd been weeping gently, dabbed at her eyes with a white handkerchief as they took their turn.

"Miss Smith?" Haley said.

Lara Smith's fragility suddenly hardened. "What are you doing here?"

"The same as everyone else, I suspect," Haley said. "To pay our respects."

"You didn't even know her."

"I knew her," Samantha said. "I had a very nice meeting with her about a month ago when I was reporting on the death of Miss St. James. I witnessed the signing of her will. Apparently, she'd just revised it."

"Is that so?" Miss Smith said.

"With Mrs. Meadows as a grandmother, I'm surprised you had to work at Filene's," Haley said, hoping her question sounded complimentary and not accusatory.

"Grandma believed I needed to know what it meant to work for a living. It builds character." Lara Smith's look of bereavement fell over her features like the Shubert Theatre curtain. "I do appreciate that you came, Dr. Higgins, Miss Hawke. Thank you. Now, there are others behind you waiting."

CHAPTER TWENTY-THREE

"Where are we going?"

Haley had intended to go straight home after her friendship duty of attending the funeral with Samantha, but instead, she pointed her DeSoto toward the police station.

Ignoring Samantha's question, she said, "Something has always bothered me about the arrest of Rees Johnson for these crimes."

"Why?" Samantha said. "He had motive and opportunity. And I thought he'd confessed."

"He said he was guilty of murder in his heart."

"It's poetic," Samantha said, "I'll give him that, but it's still a confession of murder."

"He equated hatred with murder."

"The two often go together."

"His religious beliefs made him think otherwise. One can hate and not murder."

Samantha grabbed Haley's arm. "You think they arrested the wrong guy!"

"I don't know."

"You think it's Miss Smith!"

"*I don't know*, Samantha. It's why we need to talk to Detective Brock."

Fortunately, the detective was at the precinct. When he saw them standing in the doorway of his office, he jumped to his feet with a smile of good fortune on his face. "To what do I owe the pleasure?"

Haley and Samantha each sat in one of the two empty wooden chairs facing Detective Brock's desk. He hitched up his pant legs before lowering himself into his chair.

Getting straight to it, Haley said, "Did you get a chance to track Veronica St. James's finances?"

"As a matter of fact, we did," Detective Brock said. "It appeared that she cashed a check from Mr. Kibble, but it was only one time, so no evidence of blackmail payments." He scratched his temple. "At least not with him."

Haley leaned in. "With whom, then?"

"Strangely, it appears Miss St. James may have been blackmailing Mrs. Sophia Meadows."

"The actress blackmailing the producer?" Samantha said. "What on earth could she have had on her?"

"I had my men go through Mrs. Meadows's matters with a fine-tooth comb. It appears she came from very humble beginnings, impoverished really, and worked as an actress."

"She was an actress?" Samantha said, with a look of surprise. "I'd never have guessed it by the way she spoke."

"Actresses in Mrs. Meadows's day were considered in the same category as a common prostitute, and the playhouse where Mrs. Meadows worked—she was Sophia Miller then—was little more than a brothel." Detective Brock paused, then added, "And there are those who are still alive who claim she gave birth to an illegitimate son."

Samantha clicked her tongue. "The plot thickens."

"I'm guessing Miss St. James had found this out," Haley said, addressing the detective, "and blackmailed her about it."

Detective Brock rubbed his chin as he nodded. "It appears so."

"I met Mrs. Meadows," Samantha said. "Going through the trouble a person had to go through to jimmy the prop knife and do it without being seen would've been impossible for her. She was old and frail."

"Impossible for her," Haley said, "but not for her granddaughter, who I presume is the offspring of this child."

Detective Brock tossed a pencil onto the top of his desk. "What are you suggesting, Doctor?"

"Miss Smith had means and opportunity. And now we know she had motive."

"Protecting her grandmother's wealth?"

Haley shook her head. "Protecting her inheritance."

"And what about Miss Priestley?" Detective Brock asked. "Why would Miss Smith kill her?"

"Oh," Samantha started, "I know."

Haley and the detective stared at Samantha with interest.

"When I was wrapping up the story, I spoke to Mr. Kibble. He said Miss Smith wanted to be Miss Priestley's dresser, but that Miss Priestley hadn't wanted any of Miss St. James's castoffs."

"And don't forget Rees Johnson's story for why he and Miss Priestly had fought," Haley added. "Apparently she knew all along who had tampered with the knife."

Detective Brock leaned on his desk, his hands clasped. "What we're missing is proof. Everything you've brought to me is circumstantial. Not to mention, the theory puts me in the uncomfortable position of having arrested an innocent man. Twice."

"If Lara Smith killed two women who she perceived were keeping her from getting what she wanted," Haley said, "who's to say she wouldn't have killed a third?"

Samantha gasped. "You're suggesting she killed her grandmother too?"

"Maybe she was tired of waiting?"

Haley explained to Detective Brock, "At today's

funeral, Miss Smith shared that her grandmother believed she needed to know what it was like to work for a living."

"Sophia Meadows was elderly," Samantha said. "She was bound to pass away eventually. It seems drastic."

"Maybe *eventually* wasn't soon enough for Lara Smith," Haley said. She shot Detective Brock a pointed look. "A postmortem would settle the issue."

"They're putting her in the ground as we speak," Samantha said quickly.

"We'd have to rush to the cemetery and stop the interment before the grave is filled in." Haley stared at Detective Brock. "It's your call, Detective."

The detective rubbed the back of his neck, exhaling deeply. "As much as I hate to disturb the dead, I won't be able to rest easy until I know for certain who the real killer is."

CHAPTER TWENTY-FOUR

They arrived at the graveyard with a team of men and their shovels. A field of tombstones, made to look brighter and whiter on such a sunny day, seemed almost beautiful, marred only by the group of mourners dressed in black, looking like an enormous cavity. Haley searched for faces amongst the black dresses. When she spotted the granddaughter, she started toward the cluster.

"Miss Smith!"

Lara Smith scowled when she registered Haley's presence. "What are you doing here?" she snarled. "This is a private affair."

"Not for long, I'm afraid," said Detective Brock, who'd stepped in behind Haley. "I'm officially bringing this burial to a stop."

Miss Smith's gaze moved to the rest of the men

who'd gathered behind Haley, shovels in hand. She snarled. "Don't you dare!"

"I'm afraid we must, Miss Smith," Haley said. "We have good reason to believe that your grandmother might not have died from natural causes."

"That's ridiculous!" Miss Smith's nostrils flared, a wild animal caught in a snare. "I demand that you leave this instant."

Haley nodded at the men, and they began shoveling, undoing the work that'd been so recently done.

"Stop! Please!" Miss Smith cried. She skipped about in an erratic dance, as if to music only she could hear. "You're making a mess of things."

Haley gripped Miss Smith's elbow, attempting to move the irate woman out of harm's way, but the action just made her more violent. Thrashing her arms, she managed to clip Haley on the side of the head.

Samantha, witnessing it all, rushed to Haley's side. "Are you all right?"

"I am, but Miss Smith clearly isn't."

Screeching like a wild animal, Miss Smith threw herself at the men, pushing and shoving. She grabbed on to one man's shovel, refusing to release it.

"Let go, miss," the man shouted. "I'm just doin' my job!"

"There is something very wrong with her," Samantha said.

Haley agreed. She had her black bag with her and

quickly put together a sedative in a syringe. "Help me hold her," she said.

Keeping the syringe out of sight, Haley and Samantha rushed to help the assaulted man.

"Do somethin'!" he said. "I'd hate to hit a woman, but I will."

"Miss Smith?" Haley said.

"Go away! Or I'll kill you too!"

Detective Brock and Samantha each took one of Miss Smith's arms, diverting the distraught woman's attention long enough for Haley to administer the sedative. The shock of the needle poke stilled Miss Smith, and shortly afterward, she relaxed into Haley's arms.

"Help me get her to my car," Haley told the man who'd recovered his shovel. "I'll be at the morgue when you get there with Sophia Meadows's body."

Detective Brock stayed behind to oversee the removal of Mrs. Meadows's casket while Haley and Samantha drove Miss Smith to the hospital and admitted her. Samantha took her leave, needing to check in on Talia and give an update to her boss. Once Haley was confident her patient was comfortable in bed and deeply sleeping, she returned to the morgue.

When the body arrived, Haley sent blood samples from Mrs. Meadows to the laboratory and waited impatiently for the results to come back. Hours later, when they finally did, she phoned Detective Brock.

"We have the results, Detective. Mrs. Meadows had high amounts of arsenic in her system. She was most definitely murdered."

CHAPTER TWENTY-FIVE

With a smug look on her face, Samantha made a show of putting a crisp, clean sheet of paper in her typewriter and went to work. You'd have thought the guys would've stopped underestimating her by now.

"Three murders?" Fred Hall spouted. Samantha ignored him, and Johnny answered. "The two actresses from that play and the producer."

Fred harrumphed as if the murder of three theater people was a second-rate story.

Johnny sauntered to Samantha's desk and leaned against it with his back to the other guys in the room. He wore crisp slacks with a well-pressed crease, a white shirt with the sleeves rolled up to his elbow, and a black tie which hung crookedly from his neck. His hair, parted neatly on the side, was combed and oiled, and he wore a musky scent that belied a casual approach to life. The effect made Samantha's heart race, her neck sweat, and her knees turn to Jell-O.

Drat the man!

"Don't mind them, doll," Johnny said easily. "They don't like being shown up by a skirt, but I know you're a dang good reporter."

Samantha stilled and caught his eyes, unable to keep the surprise from her face. "Thanks, Johnny. That means a lot."

Johnny grinned his maddeningly adorable, crooked grin. "After me, I'd say you're one of the best." Chuckling, he pushed away from her desk, scooped up his camera, and left the pit in the direction of the dark room.

A bloom of warmth filled Samantha's chest. *The banter is back. Maybe, just maybe, there's a chance—*

The telephone on Johnny's desk rang. Samantha glanced around the room, and when no one moved, she said loud enough that everyone could hear her over the loud din. "Anyone gonna get that? Take a message for Johnny?"

When she got nothing but blank stares or furrowed brows, Samantha scooted over to Johnny's desk. *I'm just being a friend, no, not a friend, a courteous coworker.* "Hello, Johnny Milwaukee's desk." Samantha picked up a pencil and poised her hand over the closest notepad.

A female voice pierced through the receiver. "Who's this? Where's Johnny?"

Samantha had a sinking feeling that it was Johnny's

lady friend on the other end. "Mr. Milwaukee is engaged elsewhere. Can I take a message?"

"Yeah, sure. Tell him I'll be late for our date. I won't be ready until seven."

The pencil in Samantha's hand froze. She deeply regretted answering Johnny's telephone, especially since she now found herself in the position of his personal secretary—no backing out now.

"I'll make sure he gets it."

"Say, when did he get a secretary? He never told me about no secretary."

"I'm not his sec—" Samantha became aware of the eyes in the room on her and the smirk on Fred Hall's face. "If there's nothing else, I've gotta go."

Samantha didn't wait for the girlfriend to give her more to record. Begrudgingly, Samantha jotted down the note. Her face flushed with embarrassment as if the men in the room could read her mind. With her shoulders back, she walked to her desk and focused on the story about Lara Smith and what she should've been doing in the first place.

When Johnny got back, he saw the note and stared at Samantha. Of course he knew her handwriting, so she might as well own up. Removing the sheet of paper from her typewriter, she headed to Mr. August's office. At Johnny's bewildered look, she simply said, "You're welcome."

Making her way to the editor's office, she waited for some quip from Johnny, and though none came, she resisted the urge to look back to see if he was watching her.

Mr. August signed off on the story, and she delivered it to Inky in composing.

After she settled into her chair, eager to fulfil her promise to Mrs. Meadows to write a sensational piece on her life. She wished she'd gotten to that second visit where Mrs. Meadows had promised to relay her life story, but Samantha had already known quite a bit and could find out more with Patty's help.

It turned out there were plenty of archived stories on the woman. Lara Smith's confession had included many tidbits about her grandmother's life, including the sad fact that she'd given her illegitimate son to distant relatives to raise and had washed her hands of him. This meant she hadn't wanted anything to do with Lara until she needed her help to solve a blackmail problem—a murder in exchange for riches. Mrs. Meadows had promised her estranged granddaughter a full inheritance if she killed Veronica St. James.

Samantha would never have guessed the darkness of the elderly woman's heart. It just went to show how you could never really know a person.

She started typing:

A prominent figure in Boston's society, Mrs. Sophia Meadows was known for her extravagant lifestyle and social influences, a rare woman of power. She had a reputation for being generous, especially as a patron of the arts,

*but many will be surprised to learn of her humble begin-
nings. They will be intrigued by this true rags-to-riches tale
that unfortunately led to murder.*

Born in 1854 in the rough side of New York . . .

THE EUPHORIA HALEY always felt when investigating a
case and solving one was starting to ebb away. Lara
Smith had confessed to the killings—the old lady owed
her, the stupid actress tried to blackmail her—and now
her lawyers were pleading insanity. Rees Johnson had
been released from custody, and Haley had arranged
for him to go into a care home like those set up for
soldiers who suffered from shock after the war. Mr.
Johnson needed peace, quiet, and compassion to
recover first from the loss of his brother and then from
being wrongly accused of murder.

Haley winced as she recalled a recent run-in with
Mrs. Cooper and her frosty reception. "My Brian has
moved away," she'd said with a note of bitterness. "His
reputation in Boston now in tatters."

There wasn't much Haley could do about that.
Sometimes solving murders came with collateral
damage, but Mr. House hadn't been completely innocent when it came to his treatment of women in
general and Miss Priestly and Miss St. James in particular. Quite likely, he'd been well on his way to ruining
his own reputation.

Mrs. Meadows was buried, though the legacy she left behind probably differed significantly from what she had hoped.

Haley and Detective Brock had gone for dinner once after the case closed, and Haley had to admit she had enjoyed herself. Something was endearing about the way the man blundered about, yet at the same time, his mind was keen. His gaze never grew blank when she discussed the growing field of forensic science, and Haley suspected he'd been reading up on it just to keep pace with her.

However, she wondered how long it would be before she'd see him again without a new case to force a crossing of paths. Then, as if thinking about him conjured him up, the morgue telephone rang and he was on the other end.

"Doctor," he said. "I've got an interesting case on my desk. A little different from your usual dead body."

"Oh? How so?"

"Bones. Found at King's Chapel crypt."

"Finding bones in a crypt is hardly unusual.," Haley stated. "Some of those bones have been there for over two hundred years."

"That's the thing. These bones aren't old. The victim appears to be, uh, mummified."

Haley's brows jumped. "How intriguing. Should I meet you there?"

"I was hoping you'd say that."

The line went dead before Haley could say goodbye.

She'd learned not to take such abrupt behavior personally. She grabbed her purse and started for the door, calling to Dr. Martin over her shoulder. "I'm heading to King's Chapel. I could be a while."

If you enjoyed reading *Death on Tremont Row* please help others enjoy it too.

Recommend it: Help others find the book by recommending it to friends, readers' groups, and discussion boards.

Suggest it to your local librarian.

Review it: Please tell other readers why you liked this book by reviewing it at leestraussbooks.com

** Please do not use spoilers in your review**

Don't miss the next Higgins & Hawke mystery!

DEATH AT KING'S CHAPEL
A Higgins & Hawke Mystery #6

Death is so cryptic!

In 1932, Boston's chief medical examiner, Dr. Haley Higgins is called to view bones at the crypt at King's Chapel and King's Chapel Burying Ground. Finding old bones in a crypt isn't unusual, but finding new bones is! Together with her good friend and investigative journalist Samantha Hawke and in co-operation with the police, Haley works to unravel the mystery behind the lost soul abandoned in the crypt. Who was the victim and why was the body left in the crypt?

Suspects range from caretakers at King's Chapel, to

members of the Freedom Trail historical society, to local government officials.

As the mystery unravels, it's clear to Haley that they're dealing with a sinister mind and a culprit who wouldn't stop at killing again.

Shop at leetraussbooks.com

ABOUT THE AUTHOR

Lee Strauss is a USA TODAY bestselling author of The Ginger Gold Mysteries series, The Higgins & Hawke Mystery series, The Rosa Reed Mystery series (cozy historical mysteries), A Nursery Rhyme Mystery series (mystery suspense), The Light & Love series (sweet romance), The Clockwise Collection (YA time travel romance), and young adult historical fiction with over a million books read. She has titles published in German and French, and a growing audio library.

When Lee's not writing or reading she likes to cycle, hike, and stare at the ocean. She loves to drink caffè lattes and red wines in exotic places, and eat dark chocolate anywhere.

For more info on books by Lee Strauss and her social media links, visit leestraussbooks.com.

Discuss the books, ask questions, share your opinions. Fun giveaways! Join the Lee Strauss Readers' Group on Facebook for more info.

Love the fashions of the 1920s? Check out Ginger Gold's Pinterest Board!

Did you know you can follow your favourite authors on Bookbub? If you subscribe to Bookbub — (and if you don't, why don't you? - They'll send you daily emails alerting you to sales and new releases on just the kind of books you like to read!) — follow me to make sure you don't miss the next Ginger Gold Mystery!

www.leestraussbooks.com
leestraussbooks@gmail.com

MORE FROM LEE STRAUSS

Shop at leestraussbooks.com

GINGER GOLD MYSTERY SERIES (cozy 1920s historical)

Cozy. Charming. Filled with Bright Young Things. This Jazz Age murder mystery will entertain and delight you with its 1920s flair and pizzazz!

Murder on the SS Rosa

Murder at Hartigan House

Murder at Bray Manor

Murder at Feathers & Flair

Murder at the Mortuary

Murder at Kensington Gardens

Murder at St. George's Church

The Wedding of Ginger & Basil

Murder Aboard the Flying Scotsman

Murder at the Boat Club

Murder on Eaton Square

Murder by Plum Pudding

Murder on Fleet Street

Murder at Brighton Beach

Murder in Hyde Park

Murder at the Royal Albert Hall

Murder in Belgravia

Murder on Mallowan Court

Murder at the Savoy

Murder at the Circus

Murder in France

Murder at Yuletide

Murder at Madame Tussauds

Murder at St. Paul's Cathedral

LADY GOLD INVESTIGATES (Ginger Gold companion short stories)

Volume 1

Volume 2

Volume 3

Volume 4

Volume 5

HIGGINS & HAWKE MYSTERY SERIES (cozy 1930s historical)

The 1930s meets Rizzoli & Isles in this friendship depression era cozy mystery series.

Death at the Tavern

Death on the Tower

Death on Hanover

Death by Dancing

Death on Tremont Row

THE ROSA REED MYSTERIES

(1950s cozy historical)

Murder at High Tide

Murder on the Boardwalk

Murder at the Bomb Shelter

Murder on Location

Murder and Rock 'n Roll

Murder at the Races

Murder at the Dude Ranch

Murder in London

Murder at the Fiesta

Murder at the Weddings

A NURSERY RHYME MYSTERY SERIES(mystery/sci fi)

Marlow finds himself teamed up with intelligent and savvy Sage Farrell, a girl so far out of his league he feels blinded in her presence - literally - damned glasses! Together they work to find the identity of @gingerbreadman. Can they stop the killer before he strikes again?

Gingerbread Man

Life Is but a Dream

Hickory Dickory Dock

Twinkle Little Star

LIGHT & LOVE (sweet romance)

Set in the dazzling charm of Europe, follow Katja, Gabriella, Eva, Anna and Belle as they find strength, hope and love.

Love Song

Your Love is Sweet

In Light of Us

Lying in Starlight

PLAYING WITH MATCHES (WW2 history/romance)

A sobering but hopeful journey about how one young German boy copes with the war and propaganda. Based on true events.

A Piece of Blue String (companion short story)

THE CLOCKWISE COLLECTION (YA time travel romance)

Casey Donovan has issues: hair, height and uncontrollable trips to the 19th century! And now this ~ she's accidentally taken Nate Mackenzie, the cutest boy in the school, back in time. Awkward.

Clockwise

Clockwiser

Like Clockwork

Counter Clockwise

Clockwork Crazy

Clocked (companion novella)

<u>Standalones</u>

Seaweed

Love, Tink